SERAFINA CROLLA is a wife, mother and grandmother who lives between Edinburgh and Val' Comino in the province of Frosinone in Italy. Born in Picinisco in the foothills of the Abruzzi mountains, the daughter of a shepherd, she has lived an unusual life.

Domenica

A girl from Monte Cassino

SERAFINA CROLLA

Luath Press Limited
EDINBURGH
www.luath.co.uk

First published 2022

ISBN: 978-1-80425-069-3

The author's right to be identified as author of this book under
the Copyright, Designs and Patents Act 1988 has been asserted.

Typeset in 12 point Sabon by Lapiz

*I want to dedicate this book to my husband,
Bruno. It is his family story.*

Acknowledgements

I WANT TO thank my son, Remo, and his partner, Roland Ross, for their help in producing this book and also *The Wee Italian Girl*. I could not have done it without their help.

I also want to thank my grandchildren Lia and Matteo for their help with the computer, and Erica: she is always ready to listen to my stories.

With love and gratitude to them all.

PART ONE

The Lean Years, 1953–54

CHAPTER I
The Quarrel

SHE WALKED OUT of the house. The chores done for today. She untied her apron, wiped her hands and face, took a deep breath, and threw the apron on a bench beside the front door. She thought she would get some fresh air, cool down a little before she went to bed. But the evening was so still, there was no air, no breeze.

She decided to walk up the hill, maybe it was cooler there? She walked a little, exhausted; she wanted the air but not the walk. So, she stopped, took a couple of deep breaths and was about to turn back and go home when, in the field of corn next to her, she could see something moving towards her. She picked up a stone ready to throw, thinking it was a badger attacking the ears of corn, and threw it to frighten the animal. They normally did not come so close to the village, but at this time of the year they would overcome their fear to get at the sweet young corn.

The animal was very brave, instead of turning and running away, it kept coming towards her. Then, out of the tall corn, a man appeared. She watched as he approached her with a smile on his face.

She returned his smile. She liked him, yes, she liked him a lot, what was there not to like about him. He was tall with thick salt and pepper hair, strong and healthy. But she knew if she was not careful, she would lose him. While she waited for him, she looked around. Was anyone watching? It was so easy to set tongues wagging. She moved to more open ground so if anyone was watching, they would see that there was nothing going on.

He moved close to her, too close. She backed off a little to keep the distance between them.

'What does it take to get some time alone with you?' he asked. 'And when I do see you, we have to stand in the middle of field to preserve your reputation. Let's walk up the hill a little, there is no harm in that surely. Come on, let's walk up the hill and then down again.'

He laughed as he said this, but there was a note of frustration in his voice. As they walked through some trees, he took her hand and pulled her forcefully to him. This time she did not pull away from him but leaned into him to return the kiss. He took full advantage and pressed his lips on her neck, his hand went by its own volition to her breast.

'I love you,' he murmured to her, as his heart pounded in his chest.

'I love you too,' she whispered as she tried to set herself free. But he would not let her go. 'Please Sabatino let me go. Please stop.'

He stepped back and looked in her face, into her eyes. He could see in them the stubborn look that he knew so well. He held her at arm's length and stared at her. She held his gaze. There was no softness there.

'There,' he said, he raised his hands in surrender. 'I will let you go! And I will not be back. I'm a man, not a boy. I want to marry you; I want a family of my own. I'm sick up to my eyeballs of waiting. I am telling you now that I'm not going to wait any longer.' And with that he kicked a stone in his frustration and walked away. He walked hastily, practically running, not looking back, trying to resist the urge to turn around, to not to leave her like this.

Domenica stared after him, her own heart beating in her chest, tears in her eyes.

* * *

As Sabatino left the path that led up the hill, he walked into the main thoroughfare of the village. The first person he saw was old Zio Bernardo sitting outside his house, leaning on his stick, a pipe in his mouth. His face unshaven with a grizzly beard that almost covered all his face.

As Sabatino passed by, the old man gurgled a laugh, his eyes bright.

'Ha,' he said. 'The path of true love does not run smoothly.'

The old man had a look of malice in his mean little eyes. Why doesn't the stupid old bastard not mind his own business, he thought, and before he could stop himself, he responded in a way that he would not have normally done.

'Fuck off, you and everyone else in this crazy village.'

As he walked on then slowed down, realising how rude he had been to Zio Bernardo. Should he turn back and say that he was sorry? He could hear the usual crowd of youngsters in the road just outside Domenica's house. Sabatino decided to avoid passing there and turned down an alley. Tonight was not a good night to join the gang – after all he was no longer a boy, right?

Every night after sunset the boys and girls from the area would gather outside Domenica's house, sit on the bench, prop themselves on stools and pass the evening. Anything for a laugh, jokes, pranks, gossip and horseplay with the girls. They gathered outside Domenica's house because there were no parents around to spoil their fun. Domenica was the head of the household. She would join in, after all she was young too. She had four brothers and a sister: Peppino, Antonia, Pietro, Angelo and Bruno. Sabatino would join them some evenings, so he could spend some time with Domenica. But not tonight. He was angry with her. How long had she put him off? Always keeping him at arm's length, afraid of what people might say.

It was never the right time for them to fix a date to get married. First, she had had to wait until Peppino got married and settled. Peppino, who was four years younger than her, had now been married for two years. I really can't leave until Antonia is married, she then said. What will people say, a young woman without parents to take care of her? Antonia was now twenty-two years old and was no nearer to getting married. Last summer she was courting Alfonso, a young man from Fontitune, but Domenica had not let it continue because he had a bad reputation. Apparently, he was always in trouble with this woman or that woman, even married women.

By sheer force and strength of character, Domenica had made Antonia finish with him. She was always watching her, where she was, who was she with. Telling her brothers to take care of their sister. It was always Domenica's way or no other way. She had been in control of her siblings for too long. Sabatino wondered what she would be like if they ever did get married. Would she control him too? She was headstrong. He had tried more than once to finish with her, but he would always go back. He did love her – even now, though he was angry and hurt, he was fighting the feeling to go back.

He walked on through the village, he could see and hear folk in their homes, big families sitting around their tables for their evening meal. He was feeling hungry himself, but it would take him half an hour to walk down the valley to his house.

Sabatino was going past the last dwelling of the village, an old house that no one lived in, when he was surprised to see a light coming from the front door. The door was open, so he stopped to look inside. He could see three men preparing a meal.

One of the men looked at him and said, '*Buona sera*, come in and sit down, we are just about to eat, there is a plate for you too, if you are hungry.'

Sabatino looked around. The place was like a stable, not fit for men to live in. He refused the offer, saying that he was on his way home and his parents were waiting for him. This was the polite thing to say, so he thanked them and asked, 'Who are you and what are you doing in this God forsaken village? Did you ask the owner of this house if you could stay here?'

'Yes,' one of them said. 'Our foreman has made arrangements. We are going to be working in this area for at least six months.' He held out his hand, 'My name is Giovanni Carpico, what's yours?'

Sabatino introduced himself and looked at the two other men. Giovanni said, 'This is Antonio and that is Elio.'

'You said you are staying here for six months,' Sabatino said. 'What do your wives say about that?'

'We are not married,' replied Giovanni, 'although Antonio has a girl. But Elio and I are both free. We have seen some really pretty girls here.' He said this with a laugh and Sabatino laughed too, thinking to himself, they should be so lucky. The girls in this village were no easy pick up.

Then Antonio put three plates filled high with steaming spaghetti on the table, and the men sat down to eat.

'I am going away, but I will see you around,' Sabatino told them. 'I live down the valley in Casale. But I have a girlfriend here and come often.' Then he thought to himself, *but I won't be coming for a while.* He was going to teach her a lesson. And with that he bid his farewells and started walking. It was dark, but it did not matter. He knew every rock in the road.

As he made his way home his thoughts went to Domenica. He did not know what to think of her, he was angry and frustrated. Then his thoughts went to Giovanni, the man he had just met. Wasn't he generous offering dinner? What a lovely guy.

CHAPTER 2

Resti

THE DAY AFTER Sabatino had left her alone on the hillside, Domenica was in the kitchen peeling some potatoes. She was making pasta and potatoes for the midday meal. In a pot, she had already put some pork belly to fry with garlic, onions and herbs.

Just then her sister-in-law, Resti, Peppino's wife, walked in. She had been at her mother's house since the early morning. She spent a lot of time at her mother's, especially when Peppino was at the high pastures doing his shift, guarding the communal herd of sheep. Domenica looked at her from head to toe, something that she often did with Resti. As usual she looked as fresh and clean as a rose. Not a thing you could say of many folk from these parts, Domenica thought. After all, in order to have a wash, the water needed to be taken from the local well and then heated by burning branches fetched from the forest. But somehow, Resti did look fresh, her clothes clean and mended. Her hair was always just so and smelled of soap.

Once, they'd had crossed words. Resti had walked out of her bedroom and a waft of perfume had followed her. Domenica had said sarcastically, with a wry smile, 'What a lovely smell, shouldn't you save your money for essentials and a house of your own even?'

Resti quietly answered, 'I have not wasted any money. I made the perfume myself, with wildflowers and a couple of spoonfuls of oil. Nonna Restituta showed me how to do it.'

Resti's grandmother, Restituta was born in Paris; she grew up there until the age of sixteen. Then at the turn of the century, they returned to La Ciociara. Things had been getting nasty in Paris, many people had spoken of war. So, the family had returned to the village. But the girl had never forgotten her first years in a metropolis and was always filling her first granddaughter with many ideas that the rest of the folk found very strange.

Resti now took the lid off the pot to see what was cooking, the smell was mouth-watering, but she could see it was just pasta and potatoes. So, this would be Peppino's homecoming meal after his week-long shift in the mountains.

She put a pot of water to heat by the fire so that he could wash when he came home, and walked into her room which was just next to the kitchen. The house had three rooms with the front door leading straight into the kitchen, then a room on each side. The bedroom that was Resti and Peppino's used to be a storage room. It had been cleared out when they were married. Domenica and Antonia slept in the other room. In a corner of the kitchen was a wooden ladder which led up to the attic where Pietro, Angelo and Bruno slept. Under the house, as was the norm, were stables.

Resti got her husband's change of clothes ready. She put them on the bed and passed her hand over them. She could see them on his body, tall and lean. She imagined the smell of his skin, the touch of his hands as he stroked her face. The look in his eyes after seven long days. She thought of the poor meal he'd be given: pasta and potatoes. What kind of food was that to put before a man after a week of working hard and making do? She wished she had a place of her own, just one room or two would be enough to start with as long as they had their own front door and a fireplace. She would make it really nice, keep it as clean as she could, would wash as many clothes as she wanted to without being told that she was wasting soap! When Peppino came home she would make him egg pasta with a rich tomato sauce and a sausage in it just for him.

Peppino would be home any time now. She looked at herself in the mirror and passed her hand over her hair before dabbing a drop of perfumed oil behind her ears. She then heard Domenica calling her and went back into the kitchen.

Domenica looked at her from head to toe and said, 'If you've finished making yourself beautiful, go and get some water and do not take all day, there are things to be done.'

Resti picked up the pitcher and went to fetch water. Domenica was one to talk, she thought. Whenever she went somewhere, she would forget to come back. She loved to gossip, she would talk to anyone about anything.

Resti walked quickly, the well was only five minutes away. If there was a queue of people, she would just have to wait her turn. She wanted to be at home when Peppino arrived.

At the well there were only three or four people, one of them was her little sister Rosa. There was no one actually filling their pitchers, they were too busy talking. Her sister was playing with another girl, splashing around in the water.

Resti was not much of a gossip, so she soon filled her pitcher, propped it on her head and was on her way home. Resti was tall and slender with good legs. Holding the pot with one hand, as she made her way home, she looked elegant and graceful. The other women stared at her as she walked away. One of them said under her breath, 'Who does she think she is?' and was about to say more when she noticed Resti's sister Rosa, so she cut it short.

Peppino was already at home when she got there. He smiled at her and helped her to put the water down. As he did this, he could smell flowers. She took his breath away, she looked so beautiful. Then in unison they turned and looked at Domenica who was cutting huge slices of bread as if feeding the five thousand.

Just then Antonia appeared and went to help her sister. She took to grating cheese, being careful not to grate her fingers. Angelo and Bruno both walked in, the smell of food was sure to attract their attention. They all sat around the table, a plate of steaming pasta and potatoes with pecorino cheese on top for each of them. It was a simple meal but they were soon ready for another plate. They could have more cheese if they wanted.

Resti looked at her husband. If she was cooking, she would have added some vegetables or made a salad. There were plenty in the vegetable patch, but it was too much trouble for Domenica to pick and cook them. When she had a house of her own, Resti decided she would have at least salad on the table every day.

Peppino and Domenica were talking about things that had to be done.

'Peppino,' Domenica was saying, 'Pietro is ploughing the field at the Canale for Zio Antonio. I think you better go there and help Pietro, make sure that he is doing it right. I don't want to hear Zio Antonio complaining when he comes to pay, saying that Pietro is too young to do that kind of work, that he does not have the strength to plough deep enough. When we all know that Pietro has the strength of two men. And help Pietro to remove the harness from the bullocks while you're there. Take them home to water and feed them.'

The team of two bullocks had cost a lot of money, and the family hired them out to plough other people's fields as well as their own of course.

Then she turned her attention to Angelo and Bruno. 'You boys go to the field at Celino, clear the plot of surface stones, it's been lying fallow for three years. Now we have the team we will plough it. Then we will give it a good layer of manure ready to plant wheat for the autumn. And remember you are going there to do a job, not just to waste time. Put the stones at the side of the field. Then we will use them to mend the dry-stone wall. Take the wheelbarrow with you.'

Peppino got up to go. Resti watched him go and thought, when will tonight come? She got up to follow him outside, saying that she was going to hoe the beans. She picked up her headscarf, she did not want her hair to go frizzy in the sun. When they were outside, they cast a quick look around before having a quick kiss. Angelo and Bruno laughed as they passed.

The plot of land where they had their vegetable patch was not far from the house. It was a field by the side of the road that went through the village, ideal for building a house. Peppino and his brothers always said that one day they would divide the field up into four plots, and each one of them would build a house there.

Resti was hoeing the rows of beans, but she was thinking of her house, her dream house, and what it would look like. She would have balconies with flowers and an *orto* for vegetables. At the front of the house, she wanted a garden with roses, carnations as well as dahlias and chrysanthemums to use for the feast of the dead, on the first of November.

Peppino was with his brother Pietro, he could see that he was struggling with the animals. He looked completely exhausted.

'Have you had a break, and some food?' he asked him. 'You look all done in, here, let me take over.'

Pietro handed the plough over to Peppino and said, 'Yes, Zia Concetta did bring lunch. But what a misery, not enough for us all, and no wine, just water. How she expects a man to work under this hot sun, I do not know. I'm still hungry. Even for the animals, the bale of hay that she brought looked more like straw. I tell you, if he was not our Zio, I would refuse to plough his field.'

His brother told him to go home to have something to eat, then come back to help him unharness the team. Pietro was glad to do as his brother said.

When Peppino finally got home hours later, the family were all sitting at the table, hungry yet they hadn't started the meal. The food was on the table, but Domenica insisted that everyone had to be home before they could start to eat, everyone had to have their fair share, even now that food was plentiful.

She had made an omelette with potatoes and onions. There were also some greens on the table that Resti had brought home from the *orto*. She had washed and prepared them ready for Domenica to fry with olive oil, garlic and hot pepper. There was also wine and water.

At last, Peppino walked in and sat down. His wife gave him a look that said, *I will speak to you later.* She was angry with him for being late. After the food had finished, Domenica put a basket of walnuts on the table, and everyone tucked in.

'Ha,' said Domenica directing her comment to Angelo and Bruno. 'The nuts are good, you like them, but when I tell you gather them in the autumn, you are never ready.'

Just then a man and a boy appeared at the door. It was Gerardo and Natalino.

'You have not finished eating, we will wait outside,' Gerardo said.

'No come in,' Domenica replied, standing up. 'Have some nuts.'

They took a handful each and went outside, followed by Peppino and the boys. The three women cleared up before they too went outside. Resti, however, did not go outside, she instead took a pitcher with water and went to her bedroom.

Soon other villagers came to sit outside the house for a while, everyone had something to say but it was mostly foolishness.

Then Peppino said, 'On the way home tonight I met Perella, the engineer from Picinisco. He was saying that they are about to start building *le briglie*, a retaining wall in the Rava torrent.'

The Rava was a river that flowed just at the side of Valle Porcina. In the summer it was just a small river that ran down the valley but, in the spring, as the snow melted, it would come down in a torrent taking down everything in its path. It eroded the land and brought down huge boulders. Then it would flood the plain in the next valley. In the summer, vegetation would grow in the dry riverbed and goats would graze there.

'They are going to build a reinforced retaining wall to slow down the force of the water,' Peppino continued. 'They are looking for labourers, if anyone is interested?' He then got up – he was looking for his wife, he could see that she was not there, so he went inside.

Domenica, sitting outside on the bench, kept looking down the street waiting for Sabatino to appear. Her heart was heavy. 'Please come,' she kept saying to herself. Then, from inside the house she could hear Peppino and Resti talking quietly, then the sound of their love making. The boys giggled. She got up and closed the front door.

CHAPTER 3
Antonia

'ANTONIA,' DOMENICA CALLED to her sister. She stepped outside and shouted for her again. But she was not far away, she stepped out of her friend's house across the street.

'I am sure they heard you in Fontitune!' Antonia said.

'Well, I did not know you were at Carmela's passing the time of day,' Domenica replied. 'There are things to do! You know that, why do I always have to tell you? Anyway, I will not be here to make the midday meal, you do it. I'm going to Picinisco to the embroiderer to have the two sheets I bought at the market embroidered. What colour do you want?'

'What colour do you want?' Antonia answered.

'I think I would like blue.'

'Then let mine be pink.'

Antonia watched her sister as she got ready to go. She put the linen sheets in a wicker basket. In another basket, which she would carry on her head, she put in a large well-matured cheese. Around the cheese she placed small, dried ricotta cheese that had been stored in wheat bran to keep them fresh. Domenica would sell them at the shop in Picinisco. With that money she would pay for the sheets to be embroidered.

Domenica then got herself ready. She washed, making sure that her feet were clean because that was the first thing that people would notice. She put on her second-best clothes. They were old but clean, so she was happy with that. A clean headscarf, and she was ready to go.

She picked up the basket, Antonia helped her to put it on her head and she was off, telling her sister what was to be done in her absence.

As soon as Domenica was out of the door, Antonia relaxed.

'Great,' she thought, 'I can have a rest.' She loved her sister but sometimes she was just too much. 'Always things to do, always.' She was like a sergeant major. Well, that was fine when they were young. Now they were adults, she even bossed Peppino about who was twenty-four years old and married.

Domenica would always cook, and she made the bread, but she was the one that did the cleaning and washing of clothes for all the family. Resti would also help because she loved washing clothes. Resti had such high standards with regards to cleaning and washing.

Domenica had time to sit and chat, she loved to gossip. She knew everything about everybody and what she did not know, she was not afraid to ask and every time there was a chore to do in Picinisco she would be off.

'There she goes', thought Antonia, 'I won't see her until dinner time.'

She did not know if she was glad or sorry. Sometimes she thought, 'I would like to go to Picinisco. I would like to choose the design of the embroidery myself. I would have liked to see the colours available'. But no, off Domenica would go and decide everything herself.

Antonia thought she could have been married to Alfonso if her sister had not forbidden it, she had liked him a lot. He loved to play the accordion and dance. Wherever he was it was always a feast. People would gather around him, he was great fun and she basked in his presence. But Domenica had said, 'Yes, he is great fun, he loves to play and dance. He loves company. He loves to go about. And that is just what he will do after you are married. You take my word for it, like father like son, because his father is just the same and everyone knew that Alfonso's father had a lady friend in Casale that he visited. When her husband found out he shot him with a shotgun. It did not kill him. He stayed away for a while. And then people said that he was seeing her *again*.'

So Domenica had put a stop to it saying that she should not speak to him and keep away from him or people would talk, that she would be associated with him and suitable young men would stay away from her. Antonia hoped that her sister was wrong because since then she had no offers *a fare l'amore*.

But really, there was not much choice in the village – most of the young men were related to her. If only she could be like other girls, they seemed to have more freedom to go about as they pleased, they were allowed to have fun. For her it was different, because she had no mother or father. Domenica was extra strict, saying that people were just waiting for them to ruin their lives and make a bad end.

She closed the front door, deciding to heat some water, wash her hair and have a bath. She must make the most of herself – look at Resti, she thought, she looked lovely all the time, without effort it seemed. She must be quick though, to lock the front door during the day because, this was another thing that set tongues wagging. Everyone's front door was always open, people just walked in. Then she thought: No, I will not close the door. I will wash in my room. It would be more work carrying the water there, but it would be for the best.

She was sitting outside in the sun later, combing her hair. It was almost dry and she pleated it into one long plait and left it hanging over her shoulder.

Antonia went to the bit of broken mirror that was hanging on the wall, which her brothers used for shaving. She looked at herself. She was not plain, in fact she was quite nice looking, nearly as nice as Resti. Antonia thought, I must try to copy her. Then she laughed at herself, Resti was much taller than her. How could she copy that?

Shaking her head, she went back into the house and started to prepare the midday meal.

CHAPTER 4
Military Service

DOMENICA WALKED UP the steep road that led to the crossroad towards Fontitune. She was nimble and strong, and she was soon there. She hoped that she would meet someone on the way to Picinisco; it would make the time pass quicker on the long walk.

She was lucky because just as she reached the crossroads, as if they had fixed an appointment, she met her friend Maria who had her little daughter, Serafina, with her.

They soon got into their stride and as they walked, they talked about this and that. Domenica was soon asking questions about the people in Fontitune. Who had sold their horse; who was complaining about their crop; who was getting married... there was never a shortage of things to say.

'How is Resti?' Maria asked. 'Is she getting over the loss of her baby?' Resti was Maria's niece, the daughter of her sister Antonietta, she knew that when she lost her baby she had been devastated.

'Yes, she is physically well enough,' Domenica answered, 'but I don't think that she has gotten over it.

It's been worse for her because of her mother. As you know, she goes there every day to look at her baby sister – your new niece. It was unfortunate what happened, both mother and daughter falling pregnant at the same time. Then Resti lost her child and nearly lost her life. Her mother went on to have her baby with no trouble at all. It was not fair, her mother did not want another child. Resti and Peppino wanted a baby very much.'

She then went on to say, 'They really can't afford to have a child, they need a house of their own to be a proper family. They have a little bit of money that was given to them as wedding gifts. And Peppino has some money of his own and maybe Resti's father would give a little, but how much can he give? He has such a large family.'

'Oh dear, what misery,' she went on. 'The war has made us all paupers, before the war everyone was doing well in their own way. I know that there were poor people even then but at least folk that had something would help others either by giving them work or a spare room. Now nobody helps, everyone is for themselves.'

'Let's hope that the goodwill of our neighbours will return,' Maria said on a more positive note. Maria's little girl was walking beside her, keeping in step with them. She was very quiet and seemed to be listening intently. Maria let go of her hand. 'Go by yourself big ears,' she said to her laughing.

The child was then left behind as they walked on. She was chasing a blue butterfly.

'Come,' called her mother.

That morning the girl had begged and begged: 'Please, please Mamma I want to come with you', but Maria had said no.

'The walk is too much for you. Stay at home with your Nonna.' She left the child crying. Then as she got as far as the bottom of the village, she heard a cry.

'Mamma, Mamma, wait for me,' and Serafina appeared, running towards her. She was funny, she had changed into her clean checked dress, splashed her face with water, you could see where the water had reached. The buttons of her dress were undone at the back.

'I want to come with you Mamma,' she cried.

'All right,' Maria said. 'Does Nonna know that you are with me?'

'Yes, she kept calling me back, but I wanted to come with you,' the girl replied.

Maria had to laugh. She was a strange child.

Domenica and Maria were about the same age, yet Maria was married and had three children. But Domenica at twenty-eight was still not married and, according to some, she was destined to be a spinster if she did not grab her man soon.

'What about you?' Maria asked Domenica. 'Are you and Sabatino still together? When are you getting married?'

'I don't know. Sabatino wants our wedding to be this autumn and he is right, he has every reason to demand it after all these years. But I don't feel ready to marry yet. I feel my family still need me. Antonia isn't married, the boys are still young, Peppino isn't settled. How can I leave them? It would not be so bad if Sabatino was from the village. Then I could keep an eye on them. But I am sure his mother would not be happy if I disappeared every day to walk up the valley to Valle Porcina.'

Maria looked at her, she could see that she was losing the bloom of youth.

'Domenica, you have taken on the responsibility of your brothers and sister for too long now. They are old enough to take care of themselves. It's about time you thought of yourself. More than time.'

'Yes, you are right,' she said with a deep sigh.

By this time, they had reached their destination, they parted as each had different errands to run. Domenica's first stop was at the local shop to see if Filomena wanted to buy the produce in her basket. Filomena did – she bought the ricotta and wanted the mature pecorino cheese too Filomena said that there was such a large demand for the tasty mature cheese at the moment.

Domenica it was unable to give the latter to her, because it was for someone else, but she told her that she could bring her some tomorrow, and asked her how many kilos she wanted.

'Do you mind if I leave my basket with you?' Dominica asked. 'I have to go to the Town Hall, I must speak with the mayor.'

'No trouble at all,' Filomena answered. She liked Domenica, she always had time to chat. Domenica asked for a piece of brown paper, which she wrapped the large cheese in, and left.

She walked across the piazza, through the archway, then a cobbled lane that led to the church. Before she reached the church, she climbed a steep staircase which led to the Town Hall and asked if the mayor was in. The assistant said yes as she glanced at the parcel in her hands, telling her that she had to wait – the mayor was busy with someone else.

Domenica was soon talking with la Signora Assistente, speaking in her correct Italian to show her superiority, but Domenica was not intimidated and carried on chatting away as normal. After a while a woman walked out of the office, Domenica knew her and went to greet her.

'How are you Costanza, and how's your mother?'

Costanza was a girl from Valle Porcina, she had married a man from down by. Costanza looked at Domenica with tears in her eyes. 'Have you not heard? My mother died yesterday. She always said that when she died, she wanted to be buried in Picinisco. I was just speaking with the mayor about a place for her at the cemetery.'

Domenica embraced the woman to give her condolences. 'I am so sorry for poor Immacolata, poor thing, she was bedridden for so long. You did your best for her, you came and took her to live with you. It's been hard for you, too. Tell me, what time is the funeral?'

'At four o'clock tomorrow,' Costanza said as she moved to go. Just as she was about to go Domenica put a hand on her arm.

'What are you going to do with your house in the village? You will not be needing it.'

Costanza answered, 'No, I don't need it, I am happy where I am. I am going to sell it so spread the word.' And with that she went away.

The mayor called Domenica in. He knew her very well, she was always in for one thing or another.

'What can I do for you today, Domenica?' he asked. She opened her bag. Among other things there was an envelope. She gave it to the mayor to read. After a while he said: 'Yes, they are military call up papers for Pietro. It says that he has to go for a medical visit on the first of July.'

Domenica, although she could not read, had suspected this was the case 'Well, I don't want him to go off on military service,' she said firmly. 'We need him at home. We now have a pair of bullocks, we bought them as calves, we have reared them and trained them to plough. They cost us a lot of money. Pietro is needed at home as a ploughman. Please write to them and say that Pietro is the man of the house, and we cannot do without him.'

The mayor, Orlando, looked at the determined woman in front of him. He knew that one way or another she would get her way.

'That reasoning worked for Peppino, I don't know if it will work again,' he said.

'Peppino is married, he is no longer the man of the house. You know that', she said.

'Well leave it with me and I will do my best.'

'Please do,' she said as she put the round of cheese in front of him on the desk. The mayor pretended to ignore the offer she made and led her to the door.

Her next stop was at the artisan where she left the two linen sheets to be embroidered. The woman asked Domenica if she was getting her trousseau ready.

'Not yet,' Domenica replied, 'but soon, so do a good job and for a good price please.'

'Very well,' she answered. 'Bring me some good quality sheets and a bed cover and I will make something really special for you and at a good price. You deserve it after everything you have done.'

Domenica passed by the butcher. She was thinking of getting some beef. The family rarely bought meat; they made do with what they had at home. She walked into the shop and bought a kilo of beef shin. Everyone needed a treat every now and then.

She went back to Filomena's shop to get her basket and bought a kilo of salt, a kilo of sugar and three kilos of pasta. Just the basics. She would have loved to buy some coffee, but it was too expensive. They would make do with roasted oats ground to a powder with milk and sugar, it would be fine.

She was on her way home, her thoughts heavy. Sabatino had not come to see her since their argument by the cornfield. 'Please come tonight,' she prayed. She did not want to lose him. She had to make a decision soon.

CHAPTER 5
The Evil Eye (*Il Malocchio*)

DOMENICA WAS SLEEPING with her sister by her side when she was woken up. She opened her eyes and listened.

'That's it,' she thought, 'I have had enough of being woken up every night.' She turned on her side, covered her ears and tried to go back to sleep. She tossed and turned. She really wanted to sleep. She sat up and watched Antonia sleeping soundly, she looked at her in envy. 'If only I could sleep like her. Why do I have to have all the worries?' All of a sudden, she had had enough. 'Please Sabatino, don't stay away, I'm ready.'

In the morning after breakfast, all the family was out of the house. Domenica climbed the steps that led up into the attic. She opened the window as the room needed airing badly. She gathered all the dirty clothes lying about. Domenica looked around the room. Two beds, one double and one single, that Pietro slept in. The double bed was shared by Angelo and Bruno. There was also a chest of drawers on which various objects lay. Domenica's eyes went straight to a comb. She looked at it. *No, that would not do*, she thought. It was shared by all three boys. She went to the double bed, she knew which side each boy slept on, pulled the covers down and examined the sheets. She made a face, they needed to be changed.

She then took Angelo's pillow and examined it. Yes, it had quite a few hairs on it. She carefully brushed them onto her hand, putting them aside. Then a few more hairs recovered from the bed. She removed the pillowcase from Angelo's pillow and put the hairs she had collected on the pillowcase and wrapped it carefully. She went down the steps and put the folded pillowcase in a basket, making sure that she had some money, and then left.

Domenica walked briskly. She wanted to return soon, so nobody would ask where she had been. She crossed the village and went down the valley, where she could see men working on the barriers, and came to a fork in the road, one went to Casale. She wanted so much to take that road so that she could see Sabatino, to tell him that she was sorry, but she knew that she could not do that, she had to wait for him to make the first move to make up their quarrel.

Domenica took the other road that went to a hamlet called San Gennaro. The young woman walked through the small town and thankfully she met no one. She came to a rough track that went to a solitary house. All she could see was the roof with smoke rising from the chimney. *Good*, she thought, *she's in.*

As she walked to the front door, there were goats in the yard and, it seemed, a lot of cats. She called for Zia Pascuccia. The woman opened the door.

'What can I do for you? Why are you here? I know what you want, you want a spell for your intended. Come in, we will see what I can do for you.'

Domenica looked at the old woman, she definitely looked the part. Old, grey, dirty, a long-hooked nose and not many teeth. The old woman gave Domenica a knowing look.

'Tell me, then, what do you want? Someone special to fall in love with you? Let me see what you have brought me.'

Domenica put the folded pillowcase on the table. 'No Zia Pascuccia,' she said. 'It's not anything like that. It's about my brother Angelo.'

'Oh!' exclaimed the old woman in surprise, it was not often that a young woman came about her brother. 'Tell me about it then. I am sure I can do something for him.'

'Well, the thing is,' went on Domenica, 'for months Angelo has been screaming in his sleep in the middle of the night. I get up to see what's wrong with him. I shake and shake him to wake him up, but he just keeps screaming, "Let me go! Let me go!" Eventually he wakes up and I say to him. "You took long enough to wake up" but he says that he was awake all the time. Then he said that every night a witch comes to him. He said that as soon as she was in the room he could no longer move. He could see her, feel her as she climbed onto the bed. But he could not scream. She would lie on him, and he would feel as if she was suffocating him. After a while she would turn into a cat and jump off the bed.

'What is even more strange is that his brother Pietro, who sleeps in the same room, tells him that it is all a dream. So, one night, Pietro told Angelo to swap beds, just to show him that nothing would happen. So, he did that and in the middle of the night, I heard Pietro cry out. He had the same experience.'

The old woman listened intently with an amused smile. 'Oh, these young witches cause a lot of mischief. They are just trying out their power, but we will fix them. I will give you an extra strong spell.' She unwrapped the cloth. 'Let's see what you have brought me. Ah yes! A few of his hairs and a few curly ones, they are the best.' She put the hairs into a dish. Then she asked if that was the pillowcase that Angelo slept on. She took a deep sniff, closed her eyes. 'Yes I can smell her.' With eyes closed she chanted, all the time pounding the cloth this way and that as she gave it a good beating. 'The young woman, she will be feeling this,' and with one last flourish she stopped.

Domenica sat in front of her mesmerised. Then Zia Pascuccia took the dish with the hair and passed a flame over them. She picked up a small box and put it on the table. It had three compartments with what looked like wood ash in three different colours.

Mumbling to herself all the time, she put two spoonfuls of one of the powders in the dish with the hairs. 'I will put in just the tip of the spoon of this red one because it is very powerful, you have to be careful.' A few more spells and she gave the mix to Domenica.

'Now,' she said, 'put a sprinkle of this on the window ledge also behind the door, so when she tries to get in, she will be repelled and go home. Then a little on his pillow so, if by any chance she manages to get in some other way, as soon as she puts her foot on the bed she will start to turn into herself and then she will make a run for it, because she does not want to be identified. *Va bene*? And remember while you are doing this you must say the Hail Mary three times backwards.'

Domenica paid Zia Pascuccia. She had the spell in her basket with the pillowcase covering it, and before it was time for the midday meal, she was back home.

By a stroke of luck, the only person at home was Angelo. She called him in and closed the door. 'Look Angelo,' she said to him, 'I want to show you something, but it's just between you and me.'

She went on to tell him about her visit to Zia Pascuccia. They went upstairs together and did as instructed, while they both said the Hail Mary backwards, which was not easy.

'But,' she said to Angelo, 'it does not matter if we don't get it right because she said that the intention to say it backwards is good enough.'

Next morning, Domenica woke up refreshed. She had slept all through the night! She thought to herself that maybe it was just coincidence. The following night again she was not woken by Angelo's screaming. And several more nights passed before she would give a sigh of relief. The witch had been banished.

It was always in Domenica's mind wondering who had put a spell on her brother. She thought of the girls that he liked, of the girls that liked him. She thought of their mothers. She knew that there were people who were jealous of them because they had thrived when everyone thought that the family should have fallen apart.

Then she thought of her own situation, a *fare l'amore* with Sabatino, all these years and now, all of a sudden, he was staying away from her. Maybe someone was wanting Sabatino for herself and had wished the Evil Eye on her. The more she thought about it, the more she could not get it out of her mind. So she decided to act.

This time she went to a local woman who lived in the village. She was a nice woman and Domenica knew her well. Camilla had the power to remove the *malocchio*, this mysterious power passed from mother to daughter over generations. Domenica went to Camilla's house. She did not want to reveal the reason for her visit so asked for her special intervention as she had a terrible and continuous headache.

'Come in, sit at the table, I will get ready,' she said. It was simply done, a plate filled with water, a little glass of oil and a few grains of wheat. Camilla took a grain of wheat and made the sign of the cross with it over Domenica, saying silent prayers. She kissed the seed and put it in the plate of water. If the grain floated it was good, if it sunk to the bottom, it was bad and you had the *malocchio*. Camilla did this several times.

Then just to make sure that the result was correct, she would drop a few drops of oil in the water. Again, if the drop of oil stayed intact it was good, if the drop of oil dispersed across the surface it was bad. And yes, Domenica had the *malocchio* really badly.

Camilla put her hand on Domenica's head again and said silent secret prayers, her lips moving without sound. A sprinkle of holy water on her head and the ritual was complete.

Domenica thanked her. No money was given. The respect in which Camilla was held for her power was enough. To receive payment meant losing it.

CHAPTER 6

Domenica Comes to a Decision

GIOVANNI HAD JUST finished dinner, a make-do affair of bread and cheese, a little bacon and a glass of wine. Giovanni and his friends always did this on a Friday night. The next day, after work he would go home. His mother was sure to make him something special. Sunday was his day of rest. But even on his day off, he still had to help if there was work in the homestead. He was a fit young man and they always left any of the heavy lifting for him.

Then on Monday morning, he would be on his bike again for the twenty-mile journey to Valle Porcina. The first part of his journey was easy, but after that it was all uphill to the town of Picinisco, and then a further climb to the hamlet in which he currently resided.

It was hard, but he was glad of the work, at least he could put something aside. This was possible because his parents would not take a lira of his wage. It was all saved for his future. His work included breaking and moving heavy rocks, fetching and carrying under the hot sun. The squad of men were mostly locals who would go home at night, but Fontechiari where he lived was too far to enable him to do the same.

At night after dinner, he was too exhausted to do anything but sleep. Sometimes he could hear the accordion playing, he could hear people dancing. He would have liked to see what was going on, perhaps even join in. But after a glass of wine his eyes would close, his head would droop, he would throw himself on his bed and sleep the sleep of the dead.

The last few nights, Sabatino had been passing by. He would stop for a glass of wine and chat a little. He said that he had fallen out with his girlfriend, that he had not been to see her since that first night the two men had met. Giovanni would talk about himself, about his family and his village. Sabatino would listen and did the same, telling him of his life as a shepherd. Both lifestyles were hard work. Sabatino encouraged the man to talk. He wanted to know everything about him.

On this particular night, Sabatino entered the house carrying a flagon of wine which he put on the table. He sat down, Giovanni filled a glass for him and soon he and his friends were enjoying a bit of company together.

Sabatino said that it was ten days since he had been to see Domenica, he was trying to teach her a lesson, to give her the time to miss him, to understand if she really wanted him.

'As you know,' he said, 'I can't keep away from her. I came here to be near her. I know she is just up the road, so near yet so far, but I tell you, tonight I am going up there. I need to know what her intentions are, either she agrees to marry me in the autumn, or it will all be off, and I have someone else in mind if she does not come to a decision. I have been courting Domenica for years but all I get is a stolen kiss now and then.'

Elio laughed and said, 'She is playing with you, Sabatino.'

'Yes, that's what she's doing,' agreed the young man, then he shook his head.

'No, no, she is not playing, it's just that she has been a mother and father to her brothers and sister, and she can't let go. She is a fantastic woman, a strong woman and it's what I love about her. One day I will tell you her story, but not tonight. I am going there this evening to tell her what's on my mind. Come with me to give me moral support and if you see me melt like a piece of butter, give me a kick so I regain my composure.'

They all laughed but Antonio and Elio said not tonight, maybe another time. Sabatino could see that they could not keep their eyes open, they were ready to sleep.

'You have to come Giovanni, no saying no.' Sabatino really wanted Giovanni to go with him. 'Come on,' he said to him. 'What kind of man are you, you are a young man, have another glass of wine. If you come, I will introduce you to a really lovely girl, you will like her.'

Giovanni was interested in this new spin on the evening and, convinced, they finished their wine and set off. On the way Sabatino told him all about the girl he had in mind. As they passed through the main street, people came to their doors curious to see who was passing.

They had not seen Sabatino for a while and were already speculating if it was all off between him and Domenica. Sabatino did not stop, now that he was going to her, he could not get there quick enough. He could hear laughter coming from Domenica's house. He thought, 'As usual, everyone is outside her front door. How was it possible to get some time alone with her?' He was annoyed. As they turned the bend, everyone looked to see who it was.

'Look who's here,' Peppino said. 'Sabatino where have you been? Just today I was thinking of coming to your house to see if you were all right, you have become a stranger.' Peppino shook his hand and slapped him on the shoulder. 'Who is this you have with you?' he asked as he looked at Giovanni. Sabatino went on to introduce Giovanni, but all the time he was looking for Domenica.

'Where is Domenica?' he asked Peppino.

'She had to go to Picinisco. She's not back yet, but she will be back any minute now.'

Sabatino and Giovanni sat on the bench and soon were included in the group. The boys asked Giovanni all kinds of questions, as village people did. Sabatino looked at Giovanni and nodded towards some girls sitting together listening.

'That's her, the one with the big brown eyes, do you like her?'

'Yes,' answered Giovanni. 'All three of them are nice, it's really true what they say, that the girls from up here are really beautiful.'

'Yes, but the one with the yellow blouse is special. I will call her over. You can talk to her. Antonia,' called Sabatino, 'come here a minute.'

The girl came over and sat on the bench.

'What is it?' she asked.

Sabatino asked her if Domenica was going to be long and had she been missing him. What had she said about him not coming? He was grilling her for scraps of information. Then he said, 'This is Giovanni. He is working on the barriers. He is from Fontechiari, near Sora.'

They looked at each other. Antonia felt shy all of a sudden when Giovanni smiled at her.

As soon as Domenica appeared Antonia ran inside to put the food on the table. They had been waiting for her and were hungry.

The first thing Domenica did was scan the faces of everyone, looking for Sabatino and then she saw him sitting on the bench and suddenly everyone disappeared, she could only see him. He was looking at her smiling, his special smile.

Bruno walked over to his sister to take the basket she was carrying. She adjusted her headscarf and went to her front door. Sabatino was still looking at her.

'You have come,' she said, her voice husky with emotion.

'Yes, I have come, are you glad? Have you missed me? Do you want me?'

'Come in and eat with us,' she said.

'No, not until you answer me. Are you glad that I have come? Have you missed me? Do you want...?' He asked in a determined voice to show that he was serious.

'Yes, I have, come in please.'

'I want my answer tonight, before I go home. When will it be?'

She nodded her head and went indoors. He followed her.

* * *

The following morning Domenica was frying eggs and a pan full of chopped potatoes. She was turning them in the olive oil. No matter how many she fried they were never enough, everyone loved fried potatoes.

'Food is ready,' she called and just like magic they were all there. She laughed; she was feeling so light-hearted, happy even. Everyone helped themselves.

Domenica sat back and looked at them all. Peppino was sitting beside her with Resti on his other side. Antonia on the other side of her always ready to help feed the family. Then the three boys Pietro, Angelo and Bruno.

All of a sudden, she found could not eat, not even a mouthful. Tears were falling from her eyes. She did not know if they were tears of happiness or sadness.

She said looking at them all, 'Now you are all here, I want to tell you something. Sabatino wants to marry in the autumn. I know that it is not news to you. But I want to ask you what you think?'

'What we think?' Peppino said. 'Of course, you must marry him. He loves you. He has been very patient, but I think that he really has had enough of waiting. In fact, if he had not come last night, I would have gone to see him myself, to ask him over because we could not stand seeing you in a bad temper any longer.'

Everyone agreed that she should marry and not worry about them. They would be fine. In fact, Angelo said with a laugh that it would be great without her. The boys laughed in agreement and then got up and went outside.

Antonia was clearing the table. Peppino took Domenica's hand and as he squeezed it. 'We have made it, be happy, everything will be all right, everything is fine.'

Their eyes met and she said, 'Yes.' She then went on to say, 'Peppino before you go, I want to tell you something. I met Costanza at the mayor's office. I asked her about her mother's house. She said that she wants to sell it and asked me to spread the word. I think you should buy it or at least find out how much she wants for it? I did not ask the price, it would have been rude to mention such things so soon.' Domenica looked at Resti. 'I know it's not much, but it would do for a start.'

'You are right,' Resti said, 'it would do. After all, we do not have the money. In fact, I don't know if we can afford it. What do you think Peppino, can we afford it?'

Peppino answered after thinking about it for a minute. 'It depends so don't get your hopes up too high Resti. Maybe it is the wrong time because we will need the money for Domenica's wedding.'

'I have been thinking about it,' Domenica said. 'You could borrow some money from Bruno, you know he has money put by at the Post Office. You could use that money and when he is eighteen years old, you can give it back to him.'

Resti's eyes lit up, she looked at her husband, he nodded and said: 'Do you think that it would be all right, Domenica?'

Domenica said, 'Of course it's all right.'

Resti and Peppino got up to go then Peppino walked back to the table and asked, 'Is your trousseau ready? I know you have been buying things for yourself and Antonia. There is money in the Post Office so get everything you need. I don't want you to feel ashamed when you go to your husband. You do not want your mother-in-law to say that you came with just the clothes on your back. I want you to feel proud.'

With that he went out to start the chores of the day.

Antonia sat beside her. 'Shall we look in the trunk to see what there is? That way you will know what you need.'

Domenica took the key, it was hanging from a nail on the wall, and opened the trunk. The smell of camphor filled the room. They took everything out. At the bottom of the trunk, Domenica found a bed cover with matching sheets. They were beautifully embroidered with the letters MCP, the letters intertwined with leaves and rose buds. The heavy home-spun linen was their mother's. Maria Carmela Pia, and only used once on her wedding night.

Domenica and Antonia held the linen, feeling its comforting texture in silence, each lost in their own thoughts.

'Do you want the bed cover or the sheets? You choose,' Domenica said to her sister.

'It would be a real shame to separate them. On the other hand, it would be nice to have something of Mamma's in her memory. Is there anything else that was hers? Let's have a look.'

Antonia removed two linen towels from the trunk, both embroidered in the same way.

'That's it,' Antonia exclaimed 'I will have the towels and you can have the bed set.'

'But the bed set is so much more, it would not be fair.'

'It's more than fair, you deserve these so much more than me, you have to take them. I will not hear another word about it.'

Antonia then gave her sister a hug and quickly went away, saying that she was going to the vegetable patch. Any show of affection in their family was rare, although they cared for each other very much.

Domenica sat for a while with the set of linen on her knees. She stroked the embroidery, the colours still fresh. She thought of her mother, her hands touching the linen, as if she was still there. She could see her mother's hands as they lay on the bedcover. She could feel her hands as she held them in hers. She could hear her voice, weak and breathless, her last words: 'Look after them.'

All at once she found herself weeping, sobbing as if her heart was about to break, the linen pressed close to her chest, salty tears falling on it. She said out loud, 'I have done my best mamma, I think that they are going to be all right and although I am going to be married, I promise I will come to make bread for them.'

PART TWO

The War Years, 1943–44

CHAPTER 7
Forced to Leave

DOMENICA WAS WALKING beside the cart, a basket on her head full of potatoes. She was holding her brother Angelo's hand. The cart was full of their things and all the food they had in their house.

In a corner of the cart her father had made space for his wife, Maria. She had her child Bruno in her arms. He was crying, he wanted to suckle pressing his head to her breast, pulling at her blouse.

Maria opened her blouse and exposed her breast for him. Her breast was loose and deflated, she knew there was no nourishment for him, but she would let him suckle for comfort. She leaned her head back, her face pale and clammy. The child suckled, and she felt him drawing everything out of her. She closed her eyes. If only she could sleep and rest. The cart pushing her this way and that, as it was pulled over the rough road.

Domenica could see her mother was distressed. 'Mamma,' she said. 'Here give him this, it will keep him quiet for a while.'

She pulled a yellow rag out of her pocket, tied in a knot. There was a mashed cherry with sugar inside the knot. It would appease his hunger for the moment.

They were not the only people on the road, other people, their neighbours, were also travelling.

The carabinieri had arrived in the village on horseback, their whistles screeching in discordant urgency. They had been told to bring what they could and leave the village. It was no longer safe where they were. The Germans were coming and there was danger of bombardment.

At first, they did not move, everyone was waiting to see what everyone would do. Would it really be safe to move? Were they not better to stay here high up in the mountains?

Some people made preparations in case the hour did come, burying the things that they could not take in their fields. An atmosphere of panic was everywhere.

Then, one day the shepherds who were tending the communal flock of sheep in the high pastures came down the mountain, herding a small flock of sheep and goats in a cloud of dust. The news was bad. The men could not believe what had happened to them.

German soldiers had appeared on horseback with rifles and guns. They had forced the shepherds to stand in a row, with their hands above their heads. They had been told that they had come to take the livestock, the sheep, the cows and the horses to feed the German army. If they caused no trouble, they would be safe, but if there was trouble, they would be shot without hesitation.

They were told to leave everything and go home. They had no choice but to do as they were told. These few sheep that they had brought down were strays separated from the herd. The goats, on the other hand, they had managed to save by stealth. The men set off as instructed, stripped of their livelihood but when they were out of sight of the soldiers, two of the shepherds who were the strongest and most nimble quickly doubled back unseen to stop the goat herder from going to the encampment as usual. The goats were grazed separately from the sheep and the Germans did not even know they existed. They were told to take another route, through this pass and that channel and bring the goats home safe to the village. The men were waiting for them at an appointed place. The plan had worked, and the shepherds returned with some pride intact.

There was now no more hesitation, everyone was getting ready to leave. The saved livestock was divided up amongst them.

Domenica's family was the last to leave their home. Her father did the same as the rest, he dug a hole in the *orto* and buried the plough and the harness for the animal. He also buried a trunk with household things and what was left of his wife's trousseau. He made more than one pit so that if one was discovered, there would be a chance that something would be saved. He also buried a sack of wheat that he wrapped in tarpaulin to keep it waterproof, hoping that in the dark deep earth it would be good to sow in the spring, God willing, when they returned home.

They set off, Peppino herding the few sheep and goats, Pietro leading their milk cows one by hand and two of which were harnessed to the cart.

Domenica's father, Gaetano, sat on the cart to drive the animals on. He kept looking at his wife, she looked dreadful. He swallowed the bile in his throat, gritting his teeth and with the long whip he urged the animals up the dirt track.

CHAPTER 8
Gallinaro

GAETANO WAS WORRIED. His wife was very ill, the last thing that she needed was to be on this rough road in this heat. He turned to look at her and said: 'Take a drink of water, put a cloth over your face. See if you can rest a little.' Then he stopped and went to the back of the cart, rummaging until he found an umbrella. He opened it and jammed it in such a way that it would create a little shade for her.

'There,' he said, 'that's a little bit better. Here give me Bruno, you rest a little, my dear.'

When they arrived in Picinisco the square was full of people, carts, animals and children. No one knew what to do, it was total chaos.

Gaetano wanted to pass through the crowd, he knew where he was going. At one point he stopped. He wanted to find Middiuccio, he had a car and he often hired it out. Gaetano asked if anyone had seen him or knew where he was. In this moment of chaos everyone was worrying about themselves and their families. But he knew that Middiuccio was not married and had no family, perhaps he would take pity of Maria's predicament and take a fare.

He found him eventually and asked him if he would take his wife to Gallinaro in the car.

Gaetano had been down-by not so long ago. He had made arrangements to rent a house in Gallinaro, but with the cart they would not get there until nightfall. He begged Middiuccio to take his wife in the car.

'Please, she is ill and the journey will be too much for her.'

Gaetano made Domenica go with her mother and there was also room for Antonia, Angelo and Bruno. With a roar the car was off.

The rest of the family set off on the tortuous road full of people, animals and carts being pulled by horses, donkeys and mules. There were also some cars, not many, and a few lorries. The roads were not made for this kind of traffic, when there was a delay it would keep everyone back. When that happened, the men would swear and curse Hitler, Mussolini and even God and all his saints.

Once Gaetano finally passed the cemetery the road was better, still slow, but at least traffic was moving. Soon they were on the high road to San Donato. Gallinaro was on the ridge on the left, Gaetano turned off the road to follow what was no more than a track up the hill.

It was dark but fortunately there was a full moon and eventually he turned into a hollow and there he could see the small house lit by candlelight.

Domenica came out to help with the animals. She had a bucket in her hand. Once the animals were in the shed, she put some hay in the manger for the cows. They were munching and shaking their heads, as they pulled hay out of the bales, their tails swishing from side to side. Domenica sat on a stool and started to milk the cow. She pulled and pulled on the udder, before the cow let down her milk. They needed the milk so much for Bruno. But the stress of the day had also taken its toll on the beast, so there was just a little milk.

Tomorrow, she would give the cow a good feed and let her rest in the shed. She had to be careful with her so that she would not dry up. That night they unloaded just their bedding and had eaten some bread soaked in milk. Gaetano and his daughters were doing their best to make Maria comfortable and they all slept, it had been a long day.

The following morning the farmer and his wife, who owned the farmstead close by and had rented the two-room house to Gaetano, came to help unload the cart. Gaetano was already awake and busy seeing what he could do to improve the steading. He had rented the house because it had a cellar deep in the earth. He wanted to make it as safe as possible.

There were steps outside the house that led down to a door. He opened the door and stepped in to look around. Good, he thought, it had no bad smell. It was dry with the aroma of an old wine cellar. It had two high level windows, to let in some light. He would double brick them straight away. He needed it to be safe, somewhere to take refuge.

Gaetano was over forty years old, he was strong, he was never tired, he just went on and on. He was a small man, his wife a good few inches taller than him, but what he lacked in height he made up for in determination and grit. In the village he was respected by his neighbours, he was a man of good morals, he never took advantage of anyone and always helped people if he could.

When Carmine the farmer came over to help set up the house, Gaetano thanked him for clearing out the rubbish that had been kept in the house. The house had two rooms, a kitchen with a fireplace and another room at the back. The rooms were large and dry. All the children could sleep in the back room. He put the bed for himself and his wife in the kitchen so that Maria could lie down whenever she wanted and not be alone.

Gaetano told Pietro to take the animals to graze at the back of the house, which had some fallow land. Gaetano was talking to Carmine, he was telling him what had happened to his flock of sheep, about the soldiers taking them all. All he had left were two sheep, five goats, three cows and a cage of hens. How was he going to support his family with that, he really did not know. He had some money, but his wife was ill. He had to pay for a doctor and medicine.

'Anyway,' he said to the kind man who had been listening with pity, 'God will help us, we will survive.'

Cecilia, Carmine's wife, arrived and, feeling sorry for the family, said: 'Come to my house for lunch today, it's no bother.'

By late morning they had done all that they could to make the dwelling liveable. Carmine went away. After a while he reappeared, pushing a wheelbarrow loaded with firewood. He also had some wine, olive oil and a basket of eggs. He put them on the table. Maria looked on and was grateful.

'May God reward your dead and God help us all.'

The family settled down in their new abode. It was September and the heat was still unbearable. They would sleep with no covers and that was fine for now. There was talk that they could not go home until the spring. The countryside was swarming with enemy soldiers, all going to Cassino. The English and Americans were coming to confront them. Everyone would look to the sky as planes flew above. They were told by authorities to make some kind of shelter because there was going to be a great battle around the town of Cassino.

Gaetano gave orders to his family members. Everybody had something to do. In order to survive, they had to take care of themselves, there was no one to help them. In the morning before leaving, he gave everyone instructions. He would then amble purposefully around the countryside. He would always come home with something.

He would do odd jobs for anyone, or he would offer to help. He would hire out his cart and team for the country folk who needed goods transported. The farmers would give him something to take home.

He would collect nuggets in idle gossip. Firewood here, a fruit tree there. He would follow up even if time after time it came to nothing. Everywhere he went and everywhere he passed, his eyes were always particularly open to anything that would burn, firewood. He was dreading the winter in that cold house. He could see his wife in bed shivering, he could see his children with no suitable clothing and shoes to keep out the cold. The only thing to keep them warm would be the small fire.

Peppino sometimes would go with his father, hoping to find some work too. Pietro and Addolorata would take the animals to feed anywhere they could, often in the ditches by the roadside.

Antonia and Angelo were given a basket and told to go to the fields and pick *cicoria* and other edible wild herbs as well as any fruit that was lying on the ground. Other times they were told to look over fields that had been harvested of wheat to see if there was the odd ear of grain left here or there to feed the hens.

Antonia was twelve years old she would show her brother which herbs were good to eat and how to put the knife deep into the earth so that the bounty would come out intact. The children were always on the lookout for something to eat. At this time of the year there was plenty of fruit in the countryside, but they were only to take the windfalls. They would eat some and take some home. The fruit was wormy, but it did not matter, it was still good.

The children would go home and run to their mother to show her what they had gathered, wanting to please her and see her smile. Maria would try to do some of the chores, but she was too weak. She would sit with the greenery that the children had brought back and pick them clean, removing earth and dead leaves. She wanted to do something to be useful to the family.

Domenica could see that she was not getting any better, she would ask her father to call the doctor. Maybe he could give her something to build her strength up, the breastfeeding was far too much for her. Her mother should really not let Bruno suckle any more, after all he was over two years old, but Bruno would beg and beg to sit on her lap, he would cry and Maria would give in. Domenica thought she really must put a stop to it and take the child away and just let him cry it out.

There was no more milk for Bruno anywhere, the cow had gone dry, but one of the other cows was due to calf at any time, and then he could have as much milk as he wanted. Until then she would mash up whatever food they had so he could eat too.

Today, she had killed one of the hens that was no longer laying. Soon they would all stop laying, winter would come and there would be no more eggs to feed the children. She would kill the hens then, one at a time. After all, they had to eat something.

CHAPTER 9
Mamma Has Not Long to Live

AUTUMN CAME ALL at once. The weather was cold and rainy. The family spent a lot of time in the house. Gaetano had put tarpaulin on the windows to keep out the rain. The front door had so many gaps, the wind came whistling through. He had nailed some extra boards onto the door and covered them with tarpaulin which worked very well. He left the gap under the door to vent the fire. At night when they went to sleep, Gaetano would stuff the gap with old sacks to keep out the draught.

One day Gaetano had gone home to Valle Porcina to get a few things and he came back with all the blankets that he could carry. And once they had eaten they could all go to bed, huddled together in the back room. They would sleep as long as possible.

It was on a night such as this that the children were asleep. Gaetano was awake, holding his wife close to him and keeping her warm. Maria held him close, the touch of his body was a comfort to her.

'Darling,' she said, 'I am so sorry, I have been no help to you at all. The children, my heart aches for them, soon they will not have a mother.'

'Please do not talk like that, you are going to get better. We need you.'

'Gaetano, my love, I have this pain in my belly, it's unbearable. I want to scream. I hold it back for the children's sake, but I can't bear it anymore.' She cried a huge sob and then a scream.

The scream woke Domenica, who jumped up to see her mother.

'Mamma,' she called, 'what can I do to help you?'

Domenica relit the fire, heated some water and refreshed her mother with a cloth. Then she filled a clay bottle with hot water, wrapped it in a towel, and gave it to her mother, who put it on her stomach, finding some relief from the heat. She lay with her head back, her face the colour of clay and beads of sweat running down her face.

As soon as it was daylight, Gaetano walked to Gallinaro. He knocked on the doctor's door, waking him up. 'Please Doctor, come to see my wife, she is in terrible pain.'

When Gaetano and the doctor walked in the room, it was full. Everyone was up, their faces sad as they looked at their mother. The doctor ordered the children out of the room while he examined the patient. The door was closed, and Gaetano and Domenica remained by the side of the bed.

'I need to examine her intimately.' Gaetano walked out while Domenica stayed with her mother, holding her hand.

After, as he washed his hands, he said, 'You will be all right.' He patted her hand. 'I will give you something for the pain.'

Gaetano was outside with his children around him. The doctor came out of the house, walked on and then stopped and looked back. Gaetano had followed him with his eyes, then with heavy steps he was beside the doctor, dreading what he had to say.

The doctor said, 'I am sorry to say Gaetano, but your wife is in a bad state. She has a tumour the size of an orange. She has at most six months.' He put his hand on Gaetano's shoulder.

Gaetano said, 'Is there nothing that can be done for her?'

The doctor took a deep breath. 'If times were different, you could take her to hospital. But I know the hospital is full to overflowing, not enough doctors and nurses let alone medicine. I would keep her with you, and I'll give you something for her pain. Start off with just a few drops per day, because as the illness progresses, she will need more. There is really nothing I or anyone else can do.' He looked towards the house, the children all looking his way.

Peppino and Addolorata went to their father, they could see and understand. The doctor was a kind man, he was young and was not yet hardened by his profession. He said to Peppino: 'You come with me to my office. I will give you a prescription for the medicine and give you a few drops for now.'

With a voice full of emotion, Gaetano asked the doctor how much he owed him, putting his hand in his breast pocket.

'Nothing at all,' he said. 'Keep your money for her medicine because I am sorry to say, my friend, that she will need it.' And with this he walked away with Peppino following. Addolorata burst into tears, she threw herself into her father's arms, sobbing.

'Oh, Papà, tell me it's not true.'

Domenica walked into the house, also understanding everything. She gritted her teeth, and swallowed her tears, knowing that she must be strong and not give way for the love of her mother.

CHAPTER 10

A Cow for a Miracle

DOMENICA AND PEPPINO were on the road to Sora. Domenic knew the way to the hospital, but her father had insisted that her brother go with her. This was no time for a young woman to be going about on her own.

The road was full of soldiers going back and forth, carrying goods and arms to the front in Cassino. It was a dangerous time, but they had no choice, they had to go to Sora to get medicine for their mother.

Gaetano could not leave his wife; small children and livestock unprotected, so he stayed at home.

Doctor Mario was passing by, he stopped his car on the road and walked to Gaetano's house he wanted to check on Maria and see how she was. He knew that she took comfort from seeing him. The doctor would try to reassure her that, by the summer, she would be well again. She would thank God for that, saying that she could finally be of some use to her children. But from the look on her face, they both knew that they were playing an elaborate game.

When he walked out of the house, he asked Gaetano how many drops he was giving her every day. 'Yes,' he said, 'just keep giving her that amount, not too much. Do you have to go to the hospital to get it? I know that no one here has any. I hope to God that they do not run out of it. Are you able to pay for it, Gaetano? I know that it is very expensive. But there is nothing better than this for pain, it lets the poor suffering woman to sleep, that is a good thing.'

Gaetano said to him: 'I have sold one of the cows, so I have money for now. I would sell them all if there was something to be done for her.'

'No, nothing. You could take her to see a specialist in Rome, but they would only take your money. Only a miracle can save her and I'm afraid I don't believe in them.'

Later that day Domenica and Peppino returned with the medicine which was just as well because there was none left in the house, and their mother was talking aloud.

'Oh Lord,' she said 'please help me or come for me. I can't bear it anymore.'

Cecilia was there with their mother, comforting her and trying to calm her down. Gaetano took the medicine from Domenica and put a few drops in a little water. He helped his wife to sit up so that she could drink it without spilling the precious liquid. Ten minutes later the medicine started to work, and she drifted off to sleep.

In the morning Gaetano went in the stable and put the halter on one of the cows, leaving only the milk cow. With his jaw set and a look of determination on his face, he took the cow outside and tied her up next to the well. There he gave her a good wash with a brush, then a rinse with a bucket of water, and finally rubbed her down with a rag. A feed of hay and some barley followed by a nice long drink. The cow looked like a prized specimen.

Gaetano, without fanfare or even a goodbye, took his cow by the halter and led her away up the track and over the hill, passing Carmine as he laboured in his field. The landlord stood and wondered at this strange spectacle. Why was the cow a ghostly white, perfect in every way and where was he going with it?

On his way Gaetano passed a little niche set in a dry-stone wall where there was a statue of San Gerardo, the patron saint of Gallinaro. These little *capelli* were everywhere in the countryside, reminding passers-by that God was always close and perhaps keeping them honest on their daily errands. He kneeled down and made the sign of the cross, muttering an Our Father.

Gallinaro was a strip town ascending a high ridge in the middle of the valley. He had to walk the entire length of the town before reaching his destination, the church of San Gerardo. Normally there would be many witnesses to passing pilgrims but on this day the town was completely empty.

San Gerardo was well known for his miracles. Gaetano knocked at the door of the sacristy, but there was no answer. He sat on a low wall and waited, noticing that there were still some inhabitants around. He started talking to a man who said he was from Gallinaro but had lived in England for many years. His name was Ernesto. Gaetano told him why he was waiting for the priest. The man asked if he could take a photograph of him with his cow and Gaetano said that he could.

He stood next to the cow. He was a small man, not much taller than the animal, but what he lacked in stature he made up for with his purposeful gait and proud demeanour. His expression, still one of determined assignation, the photographer snapped his photograph. Gaetano sat down again, hoping that the priest would not be long. The English man sat beside him passing the time of day.

Eventually the cleric appeared for the six o'clock mass. He was an old priest, Gaetano had seen him before. Don Claudio was from the old school, never a smile or word of comfort. He was very reserved and walked as if he was carrying the weight of the world on his shoulders. But everyone said that he was a good man and took his vocation seriously.

Gaetano approached him with the snow-white cow. '*Buona sera*,' he said to him. 'May I have a word with you, Father? I am Gaetano, a shepherd from Picinisco, I am here as a refugee. I live in a small house at Colle Prato. I have seven children, and my wife is very ill, in fact, Father she is dying.'

'Yes, yes,' said the churchman waving his hand in dismissal and walking on. 'I know it's hard times for everyone. The war brings death and misery. If only I could help all the people who come to me, I would, but I can't. All I can do is offer you my prayers my son.'

Gaetano put his hand on his arm to stop him. 'Yes, Father that's what I want, your prayers. I have brought this cow as an offering to San Gerardo so that with your prayers the saint will grant my wife a miracle and make her well again.'

The priest stopped and looked at the man. He could see that he was a poor peasant, his face was weather beaten, grey hair, and hands that were gnarled with work. He said to him, 'My Son take this animal home. In these terrible times you will need it, I will say prayers for your wife just the same.'

'No, Father,' Gaetano said, 'take it and do with it as you wish. I want to do this. Give the cow to someone who needs it more, in the name of San Gerardo.' And with that he put the lead of the cow in the priest's hand and walked away.

The English man had seen and heard everything as he sat on the wall. He walked over to the priest and said, 'There are still people who have faith Father even when we are killing each other like flies.'

That night, when they were about to eat their meagre meal, they heard a knock at the door, a desperate knock that shook the house. Gaetano picked up a club. Peppino did the same and stood by his father.

'Who's there?' Gaetano asked. No answer. He shouted again. 'Who is there!' He heard a murmuring, and he slowly opened the door. There on the doorstep was a man who had collapsed.

'*Aiuto, aiuto*. Please help me.'

Gaetano's first reaction was to slam the door shut, lock and put a bar across it. This was a time of war. No one could be trusted openly like before, how did he know this person's intentions were good? Then there was a feeble scratching at the door. Gaetano stood back rubbing his beard, his family around him.

Then he thought, 'Maybe this is San Gerardo testing me, before he carries out a miracle for Maria.'

He opened the door, the club still in his hand.

'What do you want?' he asked again.

The man only said one word '*aiuto*' so Gaetano said to his son: 'Help me to bring him in, I think he is hurt.'

Peppino said, 'Are you sure Papà?'

'Yes,' he said with some conviction, 'we would not leave a dog like this at our door, we must help him. We must not let this war turn us into animals.'

CHAPTER II
John

GAETANO ON ONE side and his son on the other, they pulled the man up and slowly took him inside the house. They let him go and he collapsed on the floor. He cried out in pain and put his hand to his leg. Gaetano looked at his leg. There was no blood, but he could see his leg was broken. Gaetano gave him a little bit of wine and covered him with a blanket and soon he warmed up and fell asleep.

After the family had finished eating, they went to sleep. Gaetano also went to his bed. He slept very lightly, which was normal now that his wife was ill.

At the first light, as was his habit, he was up. The man was still asleep on the floor. He could see he was in uniform but whether he was German, English or American he could not tell. He was lying just as he was when he fell asleep the night before.

Gaetano gave him a nudge to wake him up. Was he still breathing?

'Wake up,' he said to him, shaking him. The soldier opened his eyes not knowing where he was. Then he remembered as he looked at the man who was beside him.

He sat up and pulled himself onto a chair. He spoke to Gaetano. He spoke in a strange language. Then he pulled out his identity badge hanging on his chest and showed Gaetano the name and number. The man said: 'I am John, I am English… *Inglese.*'

Gaetano nodded, to show he understood. With his hands and just a few words in Italian, John managed to explain that he was a pilot. The plane had been shot down and he had managed to survive; his hands, in the shape of wings, descending to the ground with a thump.

As soon as everyone was up, Gaetano said to Peppino: 'Go and call Doctor Mario to see what could be done for this man Don't speak to anybody about John, only the doctor.'

Domenica, with the help of her sister, Addolorata, made breakfast, Gaetano asked John if he was hungry. It was only reheated polenta from the night before, but there was plenty of it, so he was welcome.

The young man was famished, he had not eaten for two days. Domenica gave him a spoon, then she put a wooden board on the table. She tipped the hot polenta on to the board, spread it out and put cannellini beans on top and then a drizzle of oil, finally a sprinkle of grated pecorino cheese. Everyone tucked in.

After a few spoonfuls John pulled back and looked at the family for the first time. The children, the baby, the mother in bed. Gaetano had gone over to Maria with a plate of food beckoning her with a spoonful. Gaetano saw John looking at his wife, he said, '*Mia moglie non sta bene*' – my wife is ill.

John thought to himself, 'This bloody war, look what it's done to us all.' And all of a sudden he could not eat, he was taking the food out of these children's mouths. He thought of his own mother and father, he thought of his wife. Tears came to his eyes, flooding out with a deep sob. The family stopped eating to stare at him.

Gaetano left his wife and took a plate, filling it with food and put it in front of the soldier. 'Eat,' he said, giving him a gentle squeeze on his shoulder.

After a while Peppino came back with the doctor. As they walked in everyone turned to look. At the look of fear in John's eyes, the doctor said: 'Don't be scared. I am a doctor. I will help you.'

'I am an English pilot,' John replied in English, his voice trembling. His fair hair was blackened, and his oil-stained uniform burnt and torn. The doctor nodded.

'*Va bene*, let me have a look at you. Your leg is broken but it is a clean break. It's swollen but there is no break in the skin so no risk of infection.'

John understood all he needed to with some gratitude for what could have been much worse. He watched as the doctor set to work.

'Gaetano, here's what we shall do. I think you will be able to do this better than me. I'm sure you have done it many times with your sheep. Go and find a couple of flat splints and, Domenica, some clean rags to tie the sticks to the leg. Maria, do you mind if I take just one drop of your medicine to give to this blue-eyed young man because what I'm about to do will really hurt.'

Saying this he put a drop in a little water and told John to drink it. John understood there would be pain and gritted his teeth. When all was ready, the doctor pulled the leg with a firm yank and John let out a muffled cry. The opiate already working its magic. Then he put the pieces of wood on either side of the leg and wrapped the rags around them to hold the splint in position. Then he said: 'I'm sorry, it's the best I can do.'

CHAPTER 12
Addolorata Gives Him a Kiss

IT WAS THE middle of January. It was cold, the mornings misty, breath would float away in a cloud of smoke. The ground was frozen hard and cracked under your feet as you walked. It was not until the weak sun came out in the afternoon, over the mountains, that it thawed and the ground turned wet and muddy.

The children shivered doing their chores. Addolorata would go to the shed, sit on a stool and milk the cow, her head pressed sideways on her warm flank. She would start slowly, pulling on the teats gently, her breathing steady and humming to herself. The cow would relax and give her milk, warm, thick and creamy. The girl would pull and pull and when there was not even one drop of milk left, then she would let go, giving the animal a quick hug telling her she was a good girl.

She had been told by her sister Domenica how to milk the cow, so that she would not go dry; they needed the milk for Bruno and the other children. Every couple of days Domenica would mix the cow's milk with the sheep and goats' milk, and make cheese and ricotta, a treat for all the family. If there was any left, they would give it to the owner of the land on which the animals grazed.

The young, shivering girl pulled her jacket closed. Her hands, after milking the cow, were the only part of her body that was warm. She took the bucket of milk into the house then came back to the stable to fetch the cow, and also a sack and sickle. She was taking the cow to graze on the grass and herbs that grew on the side of the country lanes and tracks. The girl would let the cow munch anywhere it could reach and when she came to a patch where there was plenty of grass, she would let the cow feed and then with the sickle she would cut the herbage and put it in her sack for the cow to eat later in the shed.

She did this nearly every day, roaming the countryside. The grass that grew on the sides of the road was available for anyone to bring an animal to graze.

She enjoyed doing what she did. She would meet people as they passed by, girls would stop to chat, boys would stop to tease her. Sometimes she would meet other boys and girls grazing their animals.

That was just as it was, times were hard. Many people had been made homeless and taken refuge in the countryside, everyone doing their best to survive, counting the days until they could go home, at the same time dreading what they would find when they got there.

Addolorata was cutting some herbage on the bank of a ditch, her sack nearly full, when in the distance she could see Armando, a boy she had met many times before, coming her way. She slid down the bank into the ditch that was beside the road. She wanted to hide, but where? There was no place to hide. Too late – he had seen her.

She was still in the ditch looking for some way to climb out, without resorting to her hands and knees. He came up to her smiling, or perhaps he was laughing at her.

'Here, let me help you.' He held out his hand, and she hesitated for a moment but then gave him her hand. He pulled her up onto the road, but would not let go. He held it tight.

'Let go of my hand,' she said, her face by now as red as a summer poppy.

'No,' he said pulling her closer, 'not until you give me a kiss.'

'Give you a kiss?' she responded. 'In your dreams.'

He looked into her eyes. 'Oh you have kissed me in my dreams, many times, but I want one when I'm awake.' He laughed and she could not help but laugh too.

'*Va bene*, just a quick peck then you will let me go.'

He pulled her closer, putting his face close to hers. 'Well, I'm waiting.'

She quickly kissed him on the cheek.

'There, now let me go.'

'You call that a kiss?' he embraced her and kissed her firmly on the lips.

'You beast,' she cried and pulled away from him. He let her go and she ran to her cow and grabbed it by the halter, making her way home in a brisk march.

He was still laughing then he called her, 'Are you not forgetting something?' He picked up the sack of grass and put it on his shoulder, following her. When they came to the point in which they had to go in different directions, he called her.

'I will leave the sack here for you, come and get it. I will go away but I will be dreaming of you all night long.' And with a last laugh he turned up the hill. Addolorata stopped and looked back, 'You keep it, I don't trust you.' When he was far away enough, she went back to get the grass. She went home, her lips burning.

CHAPTER 13
Nothing Lost in Translation

JUST AS ADDOLORATA arrived home it started to rain heavily. She put the cow in the shed and made a dash for the house. She went over to her mother and kissed her. She asked how she was and got the usual reply, a smile and a shrug of the shoulders. Her brothers Pietro and Angelo were by the fire; Bruno was sitting on John's lap. John was playing with him, talking to the boy in his own language, baby talk, she supposed, was the same everywhere because they were both laughing.

The downpour brought everyone home, and they all packed into the kitchen, the bed taking up a lot of space. John was a big man, he sat on a chair by the fire trying not to get in the way. He was finding this difficult with his broken leg stretched out in front of him, afraid that someone would trip over it. His leg was painful enough without further mishaps.

Gaetano was speaking to him, but he just shrugged his shoulders; he could not understand him. John had a little Italian learned from guidebooks and trips to Florence before the war but the local dialect was a little beyond him.

After a while the rain stopped. They could still hear thunder in the distance. Gaetano went out to have a look, from the direction of Cassino he could hear a noise that sounded like thunder but was in fact bombs. John hobbled out to listen. He nodded with an exaggerated look of gravity on his face Gaetano understood things were bad.

During the night only the children slept while the adults lay awake in the stillness of the night, they could hear the distant barrage. Planes flew low overhead. Flashing distant lights that came in through the window. Maria was crying, praying to God to help them all. 'Holy Virgin Mary, save my children, Holy Mother of God have mercy on us, implore your Son to stop this war. All angels and saints pray for us.'

Her husband held her close, trying to comfort her, rocking her, praying that she would sleep. But he knew that the only way for her to sleep would be to give her a few drops of the medicine. He had to be careful. He was dreading the day that it would run out. Now that the war had reached new heights, there would be casualties and a greater demand in Sora where the Red Cross hospitals had set up camp.

The next morning John spoke to Gaetano. He spoke quickly, with some urgency. He was trying to make him understand something and was getting frustrated because he could not get his message across. He had set his hands together again as wings, making swooping and crashing noises. He looked at

Gaetano with a crumpled face as his hands swooped above and below. Was he recounting his story again? Was there more to tell?

Outside it was still raining. Gaetano took an umbrella and set off up the hill towards Gallinaro. The rest of the family could not do their usual work. Addolorata fed the animals with the grass in the sack. Peppino climbed a nearby tree strangled by an ivy, he cut some away and fed it to the goats. They would stay in all day, their father had said not to move far from the house.

When their father returned, they were all huddled beside the dying embers of the fire. Gaetano had a man with him that they had never met before. It was Ernesto, who he introduced as a good friend.

Gaetano had spoken with Ernesto often since their first meeting. Whenever Ernesto saw Gaetano in Gallinaro, he would be drawn to speak with him, finding that he liked the man very much. Gaetano also enjoyed their chats, especially when he spoke of England.

The children stood up to give the adults their seats. Gaetano asked Ernesto to sit down and soon he had a glass of wine in his hands.

'Put another log on the fire, Domenica,' he said.

'Ernesto, I must introduce John to you, who I told you about, speak and see if you understand each other!'

'Hello John, I am Ernesto, pleased to meet you.' He held out his hand and John's eyes lit up, he grabbed Ernesto's hand and shook it vigorously, so happy to hear a voice that he could understand, he was speaking at such a speed, so fast that Ernesto had to put his hands up telling him to slow down.

'Speak slowly please.' Ernesto said to him in his broken English. 'Tell me what has happened to you. Tell me something about yourself.'

John sat back and relaxed a little, he smiled at Ernesto.

'Yes,' he said. 'I'm sorry but I was so relieved that I could talk to someone who understands me. I will tell you all about myself. But first I want to speak with Gaetano. Tell him how much I am grateful that he has taken a stranger into his house. I feel humbled and honoured to have come across such good people, sharing the little they have with me.'

Ernesto translated this. Gaetano nodded and smiled. The family smiled too. They had never witnessed such excitement, and stared in wonder.

'What I was trying to tell him this morning,' John went on, 'was that it is dangerous for him and his family to stay here in this house. I know that shortly the British and Americans are making a push to liberate Rome. They have to pass through the Liri Valley or the Casilina to get there. The Germans are holding out in the Monastery at Monte Cassino. They have the high ground and will not let them pass either way. There is going to be a huge bombardment, I'm almost certain of it. All this area is in danger of destruction and what pains me is that it will be Allied bombs. Also, as the Germans retreat, they will pass close to here.' He rested for a minute and said more softly, 'I want to get back to the British line but with a broken leg I cannot go now. I would be grateful if I could stay a little longer.'

Once again Ernesto translated and Gaetano replied: 'Yes, he can stay here with us, it's not a problem. But what he says about us not being safe here worries me. What can I do, there is nowhere else for us to go. We should have stayed in our home in Valle Porcina which is higher up in the mountains, maybe it would have been safer there. But at that time the mountains were full of Germans stealing our livestock, in fact they took nearly all we had. I thought we would be safer here, although I did not think of danger coming from the sky. I have built a hut in the woods to hide the animals, if I have to. I have also prepared somewhere to hide the children and my wife. Come outside and I will show you.'

John hobbled outside. Peppino was quick to help him and offer a shoulder. They went outside and everyone followed. At the side of the house there was a pile of kindling, mostly pruning from olive trees. Gaetano removed it to reveal a trap door. He opened it and there were steps that led down.

'There is a cellar under the house, we could go there if there was danger of bombardment. I was hoping that it is enough but I'm not so sure now.'

Ernesto translated.

John said, 'Yes, that will do, as soon as there is danger we will go there. We should store some food. Put some water there and some blankets. We may be down there for days.'

It was raining again, so they went inside and made themselves comfortable. John told Ernesto that he had been on a surveillance plane that had been shot down over Sora. He escaped at the last minute with a parachute, and the wind had brought him all the way here. He had landed on the field next to the house.

'I have no way of contacting the Allied army and I don't wish to be a burden. When my leg is healed, I will go towards Cassino because that is where I'll surely find them.'

CHAPTER 14
Deepest Winter

JANUARY TURNED TO February, and the weather was horrendous, the land wet and muddy, saturated with rain. It was getting harder and harder to feed the animals. There was no fodder, hay was impossible to find, never mind pay for as the prices had rocketed. Gaetano had already slaughtered a goat so for a while there was plenty to eat. He gave part of the animal to Carmine, knowing that he would reciprocate when he butchered one of his animals.

Gaetano hated to kill what was left of his livestock, knowing that when they returned home there would be nothing left to start again. The animals gave milk, with which they would make cheese and ricotta. They would have offspring which they could sell if it was male, and keep to restock the herd if it was female. Twice a year they would shear and sell the wool. Even sheep manure was highly prized and what they did not need for their own fields would be sold.

One day Carmine came running in an uproarious panic. 'Gaetano, Gaetano, the Germans are coming this way. Quick, we have to take the animals to the hut. They are taking everything, and I have heard that they are even rounding up able-bodied young men as labourers.'

Carmine ran to his house to gather his animals to take them to the hiding place. Gaetano quickly told Peppino to take the animals out of the shed. But what froze his blood was the thought that they would also take his son.

'John,' said Gaetano, 'you and Peppino and the three girls go into the cellar, stay in there until I call you.' Gaetano then closed the trap door and put the pile of wood back on top of it.

Then he and Carmine took the animals to the hut they had prepared together. Gaetano left two goats in the shed so that if the bastards came they would be satisfied and leave.

Rather than move his wife to the shelter, Gaetano decided that he, his wife and the three younger boys would stay in the house. Surely the Germans would take pity on a man with a sick wife and three small children. For two days nothing happened and no one came. The moment of panic subsided. From their underground hiding place, they emerged squinting in the winter sun. They came out hoping to resume their normal life but now a new visitor was among them – fear stalked them constantly.

Gaetano went to do some work for a farmer. On his way he asked everyone he met if they knew what was happening. They all had different tales to tell. Picinisco had been hit by a bomb, damaging the church in the

Square. The entire population of San Donato had been told to leave the town. La Rocca, which was a village of shepherds just like Valle Porcina, had been completely destroyed. Its prominent position and commanding views brought its downfall. The Germans were pillaging entire communities, loading up their trucks and leaving people with nothing. Gaetano felt safe for the moment as no vehicle could make its way to his solitary abode. Even a horse and cart could only manage the journey with a great deal of care.

He walked to Gallinaro one day to buy some salt and sugar and a little tea for his wife. But the shop was empty, it had no produce, only some bread made with rye flour. Gaetano asked if she had any white bread for his wife. The owner of the shop knew Gaetano and knew of his poor wife. She said she was sorry, but she did not have any, not even a mouthful.

He nodded and tipped his hat. He walked along the High Street and from the square he could see the plains and the mountains. He could see Picinisco, Atina, Settefrati, San Donato, Alvito, Casalattico, Casalvieri and Villa Latina, the eight *paese* or townships of the Comino Valley. This valley, surrounded by mountains, had only two ways in and out. One, a winding and tortuous descent to Cassino, and the other passing through Sora to the Liri Valley the next valley along this part of the Apennine Range. Gaetano had been hoping to meet Ernesto, and he stood for a while gazing at the desolate-looking panorama. The fields were unploughed and no winter wheat had been sown. At this moment there was total silence as he surveyed his world. All the usual sounds had gone. No bleating of animals; no children playing; no church bells ringing; no birds singing. Was the world coming to an end? Even the church of San Gerardo had closed its doors. Had God abandoned them too?

He started to make his way home and then thought of his new friend. Although he had not been to Ernesto's house, from his descriptions he knew more or less where to find him and, sure enough, there he was sitting outside his house playing with this camera.

'What should we do?' Gaetano asked his friend. 'The animals have been in the hut for two days. I have no hay to give them, they need to get out and forage. What do we do? We are scared to go about our usual business, but we need to in order to survive. John says his leg is almost healed and I think he wants to leave. Could you come and speak with him? He keeps asking for a radio – do you have one? And then there's my wife.'

His voice broke as he said these words.

'She is getting worse every day, I find myself praying that God will come for her to stop her suffering. What she is going through with her illness is terrible. But to have to go through it in this time of misery. To see her children suffer, to worry for her family. She prays to her mother: "Mamma, Mamma come and get me." It breaks my heart. Doctor Mario visits regularly, but there is nothing he can do. Domenica does what she can for her. When she changes the bed, she gets her to sit by the fire, she puts Bruno in her arms, but she has no strength, her life is fading away. It's as if she is being made to pay for a great sin she has never committed.'

He could not hold back the tears anymore, and just sobbed. There was silence for a while. What was there left to say? It had all been said.

Ernesto put his hand on his shoulder and said: 'You must keep going my friend, you can only do what you can, you can do no more. There is talk that by May it will all be over. The Germans will be defeated. Hold on until then, I will come to your place to speak with John. I will bring a little tea for Maria. I am afraid I do not have a radio.'

CHAPTER 15
Time to Leave

AFTER A WHILE, things seemed to calm down a little, and it appeared that the Germans were retreating. The pillaging had stopped; there wasn't much left to take. They thundered past in their empty trucks mainly in the direction of Sora, Frosinone and Rome. The people they found on their way got the worst of it, but people were few and far between, knowing to keep to the back roads.

Gaetano's little house had proved to be a good place, hidden and discrete.

The weather was still bad. Gaetano had never seen so much rain. The family spent so much time indoors, in the evenings they would close the door and put a log on the fire. Carmine and Cicilia would come and bring a bundle of olive tree branches to put on the fire, and a handful of corn to pop. They would sit and talk, telling stories that the children loved.

John would sit a little to the side, playing with Bruno. John would blab away nursery rhymes in English. He would do actions that would make the little boy fall about laughing. He would shout over and over again, 'I like John.' John had taught him to say this and a few other words in English. John would answer with, 'I like Bruno.'

Doctor Mario had taken the splints off John's leg and told him to walk on it a little more each day. He would follow Gaetano trying to help him in any way he could.

John asked him how he could get to Cassino. 'Gaetano, I must go now, my leg is better,' he said. 'I can't stay here anymore. I will never forget your kindness. But I must go.' Then he made a sign to show that he had to speak with Ernesto.

Gaetano understood the urgency nodded his head and said, 'Come with me.' They slowly made their way to Ernesto's house.

'Ernesto,' said John, 'I need to get to the British line in Cassino, what is the best way to get there? How many miles is it to Cassino from here? Do you think I can get a lift?'

Ernesto shook his head. 'No, no one is going to Cassino. But I have heard that the British are coming over the mountains at Forca D'Acero, to cut off the retreat of the Germans. They will have to pass through San Donato to Atina, so you could join them when they pass this way. By tomorrow they could be here. I will come tomorrow morning and take you to Ponte Melfa, where you could meet them.'

Once home, Gaetano asked Domenica to make something special for dinner as John was leaving them. She looked bewildered as she scanned the scant food stores but she also wanted their parting to be a little special. Who knew if they would ever set eyes on each other again?

Domenica killed the last hen and put the skinny carcass in a big pot to boil for several hours then she added any vegetables she could find. She made some tagliatelle without eggs, which she then chopped up small. During the last five minutes of cooking, she took the bird out and threw in the pasta. Then she took all the flesh off the bird and chopped it up into small pieces putting it back in the pot. In that way everyone got a little of the meat.

The next morning everyone was up to say goodbye to John, who had been dressed in old clothes and a hat to disguise his light hair. There were even some tears as John hugged them all. They had been through a lot together. When John took Bruno in his arms to give him an extra special hug, he said, 'Goodbye my little friend.' With glassy eyes he put him down picking up a basket Domenica had prepared for him. He began walking away with Ernesto and Gaetano while Bruno ran after them shouting, 'I like John! I like John!'

CHAPTER 16
The Bomb

AFTER JOHN HAD left, the winter of 1944 continued, and his forewarnings seemed to become their reality. Now almost every day they could hear the sound of war coming from over the mountain. The family would stay in the house huddled together for warmth. In the morning they would take the animals out to graze close by. They would do this only for an hour or two, pursued by fear. They wanted to stay near the house.

It was late afternoon and Addolorata had taken the cow to graze by the sides of the lanes. The sun had melted the frost and it could get to the small sprigs of grass peeping out of the earth. She sat on a log, in her hands a bunch of snowdrops their pure white heads looked so delicate. But looks were deceiving, she thought. They had pushed through the thick wet mud and then the frozen ground to be the first blooms to appear and announce that soon it would be spring. She put the blooms to her nose to smell their perfume. But the girl in her first bloom of youth was dreaming with her eyes wide open. When she married, she would have a big bunch of snowdrops in her poesy, with maybe some lily of the valley mixed in because she liked them too. The girl sat on the bank, the flowers in her hand. She was hoping to see Armando, she had grown to like him very much. He was cheeky, but he made her laugh. Maybe she would marry him. She knew that he felt the same about her. Once this terrible war was over, she was sure he would come to see her, to ask her father for her hand.

She was sitting, her head in the clouds and a smile on her face, thinking of him and enjoying the countryside, the wildflowers, the warmth of the weak winter sun on her face. Then she heard a drone and a roar coming over the mountains towards Alvito. She saw planes coming over the snow-covered peaks. There were so many, she had never seen so many before. She watched as they came low overhead. She felt paralysed with fear when she saw a plane dropping bombs. Then a huge explosion which she was sure had hit Gallinaro. She felt the earth shake. She ran for home as fast as she could.

When she got to the house, her father was shouting, 'Everyone get in the cellar!' Another explosion not far away then another even closer. 'Quick, Quick Domenica, Peppino, get Angelo and Pietro, get into the cellar! I will get Mamma.'

Bruno was with his mother. Addolorata went in to get him while her father grabbed his wife. There was a hissing, then whistling. And a bang.

An explosion blasted the house. The jagged air fizzing with energy. Smoke and dust everywhere. And then, for what seemed the longest time... silence.

Then the screams from the cellar and screaming from the house were deafening. Near neighbours listened, listless and slack jawed, the passing moments endless and electric with fear. A cacophony of dogs barking and howling in the distance because these were different screams. One sound conveyed fear and the other screamed pain. Domenica and Peppino ran to the shattered house. They would never forget what they saw. Their cries for help echoed throughout the valley.

CHAPTER 17
'I Have 100 Lira for You'

ONE MONTH HAD passed. Domenica was dressing Bruno. The child was so silent and limp, and had lost all of his baby laughter. He was now a quiet child, he would follow Domenica around and would scream if he could not see her. Or he would want to be with his mother, but his mother was now so ill that Domenica did not want the boy near her because it brought neither of them anything good.

She told all the other children to wash as best they could under the circumstances and put on a change of clothes if they could find them. Domenica walked over to Cecilia to ask her if she could come and sit with her mother for a while. When everyone was ready, she looked at them. She thought they made such a pitiful sight. With Peppino Antonia by her side, they each took one of the boys by the hand. She held Bruno. She checked that she had 100 lira in her pocket, and they set off for Gallinaro.

They walked through the High Street. The doors and windows were open now, and people were walking in the streets. Some of the shops had opened again although selling what, she had no idea. Refugees were returning to their homes with awful stories. She overheard that the ancient Abbey of Monte Cassino had been completely destroyed. As she looked around, there was misery everywhere and this news only seemed to add to it. Although the bombing had stopped for now a bitter war still raged only a few kilometres away.

Domenica and the children came to the church of San Gerardo. They walked in, and found the church in deep gloom, smelling of stale air with just a few candles lit on the empty altar. They passed by the statue of San Gerardo, tapping the saint's foot, worn smooth by the countless pilgrims that had touched it. Domenica made the sign of the cross, kissing the finger that had made contact with the statue. She helped Pietro and Angelo to do the same. She told Bruno to reach out to the Saint, but he turned away in fear and just held on tight to Domenica's neck. They slid along a bench and waited.

After a while Father Claudio appeared in his tunic, the altar boy walking in front of him ringing a small bell. The family stood up. The Mass began and proceeded through the usual requests and replies. The family staring vacantly into the middle distance.

The priest raised the Host and said suddenly: 'We pray for the souls of our dearly departed, Gaetano and Addolorata, may they rest in peace in the glory of Heaven with God, our Holy Mother, and all the angels and the Saints. Amen.'

Don Claudio held the host in front of him, he looked at the young woman and her brothers and sister, tears rolling down their faces. He closed his eyes in prayer.

After the Mass, Domenica stopped Father Claudio. 'Father,' she said, 'thank you for saying Mass for my father and sister. Here, I have 100 lira for you.' She held out the money for him. The good man looked at the money. He did not want to take it, but he knew that if he did not accept it, the young woman would think his calls would not truly count for the Souls of her departed.

'Before you go, Domenica, I want to show you all something.' He led her to the passageway in front of the sacristy and there, amongst a thousand other offerings faded and new was a framed photograph of her father standing beside a white cow. 'Ernesto took the photo, he brought it here already framed.' Domenica called her brothers and Antonia to come and look at the picture. They looked wide-eyed, the little ones not really understanding but happy to see their father again proud and strong.

The priest looked at the children one by one and he said to them all: 'Your Babbò was a very good man, remember to always be proud of him, he did his best and you should do the same. Do your best and everything will be fine, and remember to say your prayers.'

The folks that had left their homes were itching to return. Maria would lie on her bed, at times she would forget that Gaetano was dead and call for him. 'Gaetano, *amore mio*, where are you? Come here the children need... Gaetano where is Bruno?' At other times she would remember everything, and the horror of that day would flood back with bitter tears. 'Addolorata my darling girl, my beautiful girl.' Then she would turn her eyes to heaven and ask, 'Why her and not me, Lord?' The poor dying woman begged to die. She begged Domenica to take her home to Valle Porcina, she wanted to die at home

Ernesto had asked a friend, who owned a truck, to help the fatherless children as an act of charity. To give his time and his truck at no expense. Everything was ready, only their goodbyes remained to be said. Domenica gave her mother the last of her medicine. Peppino came to lift his mother in his arms. She was as light as a feather, and he tried to be gentle, but he could see the beads of sweat on her forehead and upper lip, and knew that she was in horrible pain.

'Mamma,' he said, 'you sit at the front with the driver, you will be more comfortable.'

'No, no, I can't sit, I must lie down.' Her stomach was swollen, and it was impossible for her to remain seated. Carmine and Cecilia made space in the truck and put down a mattress. Peppino laid his mother down there. The poor woman was already exhausted but fortunately her medicine started to work, and she drifted off into a drugged sleep.

'Goodbye, then,' Domenica said. Their good neighbours, Carmine and his wife smiled a faint farewell, under the circumstances anything more cheerful seemed disrespectful. Ernesto waved, with promises on all sides to meet again. Just before they left, Domenica stopped, and said with all the conviction and good grace she could muster. Words taught to her by the generations that came before her. '*Per l'anima di tutti I vostri morti*. May God reward your dear departed for all your good deeds.'

As they descended the rough track that led away from the house, she turned to Peppino and Antonia who were walking home on foot with their few animals. She gave them some money and said: 'When you pass through Colle Posta go to Marco Scapaticci's house. If you don't know where he lives, ask. Ask him if he still has a bull and if it could cover our cow, because she will soon run dry, especially with the stress of the journey. We need her to calf again. Also be careful on the journey, don't stop for anything or anyone. I will be waiting for you. I would have walked with you, but I can't leave Mamma. I hope I can get more medicine for her in Picinisco. Be careful.'

She had arrived in the truck by late afternoon. Everyone who had returned to Valle Porcina came out to help unload the truck and to help with her mother. Some of their relatives sent cooked food, which was the custom when there had been a bereavement. Domenica was thankful for that.

Domenica stood outside the house. She could hear her mother moaning, 'Mamma, Mamma, come and get me.'

Domenica covered her ears as she could not stand it any longer. She ran up the hill. 'Lord what am I to do?' she cried shaking her fists to the sky. Tears rushed down her face. 'Please Lord, come and get her, and give her some peace.'

She heard her brother down below. Thank God, they were back! She composed herself and walked back quickly to see that all was well. They looked tired, but sound. She helped them to put the animals in the stable: two sheep, four goats and a cow. How on earth would they manage with that? She asked Peppino if the cow had been covered.

'Yes,' he said, 'and Marco did not take any money.' He handed the notes back to her. Domenica told them to go inside there was food on the table.

She had no medicine for her mother. When, on their return, they had passed through Picinisco, she had asked the driver to stop. She went to the chemist, but it was closed. She made her way to see the mayor, to ask him for help. He said to come back tomorrow. Eventually she managed to speak to the doctor who came to the square to look at Maria.

He pulled her aside to tell her that her mother would not live much longer, and they should just try to make her as comfortable as possible. No, it was no use taking her to the hospital. It was full to overflowing anyway. They had no beds and they had no morphine, it would be a wasted journey. 'Come back tomorrow,' he said, 'and in the meantime I will make some enquiries.'

CHAPTER 18
To Sleep and Dream

NEXT MORNING THE family were up, and Domenica gave them instructions for the day. Domenica asked her aunt if she could sit with her mother while she and Peppino went to Picnisco to see the doctor. They took two hunks of bread, one each.

The night before, Domenica had removed the linen bag which she wore tied around her waist underneath her clothes. Peppino by her side, she counted the money to see how much she had left. This was the money her father had on his person when he died. There was not much left. She put some back in the bag to pay for the medicine and re-tied the bag under her clothes and fastened it securely around her waist. They hid the rest under their mother's mattress.

They had to go all the way to Sora. The doctor was kind, and he gave them money for the bus fare but the bus was full, there were even people sitting on the roof.

'Please, please!' Domenica cried. 'Let us squeeze in, I have to go to Sora to get medicine for my mother.

Look I have a letter from the doctor.' They managed to squeeze in, standing all the way.

Domenica noticed a difference in Sora. The streets were full of people, going about their business. The shops were open, owners cleaning their windows, stray dogs everywhere, dogs that had been abandoned in the rush to get away. They walked over the bridge crossing the Liri river and then down the High Street, which was lined with shops on both sides. They then crossed the river again down into Viale San Domenico. Sora had not been touched by the bombardment, it was still intact, a beautiful little city sitting at the foot of majestic mountains and a gateway to the Abbruzzi. Domenica heard people talking on the bus about Cassino which was completely destroyed, not only the monastery but the entire town. Eventually they reached the hospital; it was true, it was like bedlam, people everywhere, some old and sick, others wounded, blood oozing out of their bandages and others not having the strength to stand, simply lying on the floor.

The sister and brother made their way to the dispensary, but the shutters were closed. What would they do now? They stood at a door where doctors and nurses were hurrying in and out. Standing with the note in her hand, asking 'Please, can you help me?' But no one stopped, they had grown immune to cries for help.

Eventually an elderly matron who had passed by them many times as she went about her business, stopped. 'What do you want?' she barked at them impatiently.

'Please I want to give this to a doctor.' The matron looked at the envelope with the doctor's name. She knew him.

'Wait here, if I see him, I will tell him you are here.'

They waited for a long time, an hour or two. Domenica thought of her mother waiting for her only solace. At last a doctor came with his white coat flapping and said: 'You have a letter for me?' He opened the letter Domenica held out to him. 'Yes, everyone wants morphine, if only I had a tank of it. There is pain everywhere. Your mother is dying of cancer. Your father is dead. Six children! Lord in heaven, help us all. Come with me.'

He walked very fast, Domenica and the boy following. 'Wait here.' After a while he came out with a small bottle in his hands. He could see the look of disappointment in the girl's eyes. 'You are lucky to get this small amount. Morphine is like gold dust these days. Here, take it.'

Domenica asked how much it was and held out some money. 'Just take it and make it last, because there is no more in the whole of la Ciociaria.'

On their way home Peppino said to Domenica: 'I'm really hungry. The doctor did not take the money for mother's medicine so can we buy something to eat?'

'I am hungry too,' she said, 'but with that money and a little more, I was thinking, we can buy a piglet.

I know where to get one because I was with Papà when he bought one last year.'

'*Va bene*,' said the boy with a look of disappointment in his eyes.

'If there is any money left, we will buy a ham sandwich to share. Now let's take the bus, we will get off at Ponte Melfa. We will walk the rest of the way home to save money. *Va bene*?'

At the stop for Ponte Melfa, they got off and started to walk towards Villa Latina. They followed the valley until they came to Valle Grande where they went to the farmer who bred pigs.

'Oh,' he said, 'I only have one left. You can look at it if you want.' He walked to where the pigsty was and as he said, there was only one. Domenica could see it was the runt of the litter, it was tiny.

'How old is it?' she asked. 'And how much do you want for it?'

The farmer named a figure.

'Oh no, that's far too much. I can't give you so much. I don't have it and there's no guarantee that it will survive. I am taking a chance buying it. I will take it off your hands for half that amount.'

The farmer looked at the girl and he remembered her from the year before when she came with her father. He was now dead, the poor man.

'You are cheeky, I can't give it to you at half the price. I could sell it tomorrow at the full price.'

'That is if it survives until tomorrow,' she countered. 'Yes, c'mon you can give it to me at that price, you have sold all the rest at a good price. Give this one to me, please.'

The man looked at the girl. '*Va bene*, take it but don't come back to me if it dies.'

He took the money, picked up the squealing piglet and put it into the boy's arms. He wished them luck and walked away.

As they walked away, Domenica saw some old sacks lying about, she picked them up and gave them a good shake then wrapped up the little piglet to keep it warm.

They walked along the high road until they came to the turning for Casale. At this turning there was an old inn. Domenica and Peppino entered and ordered two ham sandwiches. She paid and still had some money left over. Nothing had ever tasted so good, they enjoyed every morsel. They could have eaten two each.

They crossed the Mallarino river that was still ice cold and stopped to drink. They then started to walk in earnest to get home before dark. There were almost home when Peppino remembered something. 'You hold the pig,' he said. 'I know where there's a cherry tree, I'll go and get some cherries.' He went to the tree, he filled his shirt and ate as many as he could, stones and all.

Domenica ate a few. 'We will take the rest for the children,' she said and for a while they felt happy as they made their way home.

As soon as Domenica arrived home, she gave her mother a couple of drops of the morphine and thanked heaven as she slept. She was worn out, but before she turned in, she and Peppino went into the stable to make a warm nest for the pig and make it a mash of milk and wheat bran. At last she went to bed and slept all night.

CHAPTER 19

Mamma, Don't Go

IN THE MORNING Peppino took a spade, walked to the vegetable patch and started to dig. His father had been one of the last to leave the village and told his son that they would wait and hide their goods when everyone was gone, because in times like these no one could be trusted. Sure enough, all the separate stashes were intact.

He unwrapped the tarpaulin package to see if the wheat had spoiled. While he was doing this, he sensed the eyes of their nearest neighbour, Zio Silvio, watching him. And before long the word had spread all over the village that they had wheat for seed. Soon everyone came cap in hand to ask for a handful of wheat.

Domenica took charge and kept ten kilos for the family, and she shared the rest with her relatives and neighbours. As she handed out the grain she said, 'If only I had a hen, we could have eggs. I bought a little piglet, but I don't know what I'm going to feed it, I don't have any bran.'

Zia Carolina who had a house full of boys asked Domenica if she could have a little more wheat, and she would give her one of her hens who was clucking. With good grace, the deals were done one by one.

For the moment there was food, a sack of polenta, a sack of flour, a sack of beans, some oil and lard, but once that was gone, Domenica worried, then what would they eat? The cow still gave a little milk but not enough. Peppino was just a boy, but maybe he could go to Picinisco and find some work. She shook her head and put it to the back of her mind.

She went to sit by her mother, holding her hand. Domenica had just given her a few drops of medicine and she was lying quietly. The poor soul, she hardly made a bump in the bed, only her swollen belly stood out.

Domenica looked up and found her mother was looking at her. With a weariness that seemed to come from the very depths of her soul, she said: 'I am sorry, Domenica, for all the trouble I have been to you, but the merciful Lord will simply not take me to Him, despite all my prayers. Gaetano and Addolorata are waiting for me. I am nothing but a burden for you, when you have so much on your young shoulders already. I am sorry my darling girl, I am so proud of you.'

Then with a deep breath which caused her pain, she put her hand on her swollen belly and found the strength to say: 'You will look after them for me? My poor orphan children.'

Domenica could not hold back her tears. 'I will Mamma, I promise, do not worry about us. We will be all right.'

She pressed her mother's hand to her lips, soaking it in hot salty tears. Her mother drifted into sleep. Not much later she was awake again, the pain had returned. Domenica gave her another few drops, it seemed as if the medicine was not working and by the end of the day there was none left.

The suffering was not over, and during the night she got no relief from sleep. The pain was unbearable, and she just screamed. At times her mouth opened to scream but no noise emerged, she had no strength left. Her mother's sisters and brother came to sit with her. The family huddled in the kitchen. A neighbour took the boys away so that they did not have to hear.

People came and went, then old Zia Restituta came and sat with her for a while. She kissed and held her hand. 'Let her sit up for a while,' she said to Maria's brother Antonio and his wife. 'It may help her.' Antonio and Concetta helped her to sit up. She then said, 'I think if you let her stand for a while, it will help her circulation.' Antonio and Concetta moved her leg over the bedside until her feet touched the floor. 'Help her to stand. Maybe just a few steps.'

Domenica watched as her mother rose.

'That's enough now. Put her back to bed.'

Her mother was completely exhausted from the effort. She just lay there, limp. 'She will sleep now,' said the old woman. After a while she got up to go, saying: 'Let her rest now. Maybe if we all leave, she will sleep.'

She left and the others left also, and the family was left alone to sit with her all night. She slept for two days and then she breathed her last breath. There was a deep sadness, but a sense of relief, at last she was free.

Domenica held her mother's hand and prayed that they were together, Mamma, Papà and sweet Addolorata.

CHAPTER 20
Garzone

THE HAMLET WAS returning to some normality, everyone was back and had stories to tell: where they had been, what they had seen. The terrible atrocities of the war had been a hard lesson. Stories told of young women raped by Moroccans. People hiding their daughters under mattresses in internment camps. Many of the women folk were saved by their smart, forward thinking. Others told of the near death of members of their families. The hunger and the filth and how there had been no one to help. One helped one's relatives first, and then they helped you. Family was the only thing you could rely on. This was repeated like a mantra among the villagers as they looked to their still uncertain futures.

But even this was stretched to breaking point. Now that they were back, their families were large, seven to ten members in each family was common so quarrels were an everyday occurrence. Anyone who had a fruit tree would guard it, and woe betide anyone who stole fruit. Every inch of land was accounted for. If a goat was seen grazing on another's land it was quickly corrected. If a suitable split was not agreed and a tree was felled for firewood or even dead branches collected from another's land, a war would follow. Some would threaten 'going to the law'. And the foolish did. And then the law would suck every Lira they had to spare out of their pockets.

The land that people owned was just patches here and there where they cultivated wheat or maize. Their fields were small, as they had been divided many times between siblings so there were constant quarrels about who got more, who got less, who inherited the best plot, who had fruit or water. The points of view were endless.

Before the war all these disagreements had more or less been resolved. But now with the 'great misery', it was all brought to the fore as people tried to scratch a living in any way they could.

The people of Valle Porcina were shepherds and always had been. That was how they made a living. They made money selling pecorino and ricotta cheese, lamb and wool. But they had lost their flocks and now they did not know how would they survive.

They tried to resume their old way of life. Each individual flock was herded together and taken to the high pasture. Where grand peaks and valleys had previously hosted a cumulative heard of thousands, just a sorry few hundred goats and at the most fifty sheep remained.

Hopefully, by autumn, some of them would give birth and begin to restock the flock. Even if one had wanted to buy sheep, they were nowhere to be found. Some families pooled their resources and went as far as Rome and Bari to buy sheep. They were the crafty ones.

Domenica's family had a Zio called Antonio, their mother's brother, who was a good man. In ordinary times he would have helped his nieces and nephews, but now he could only help with advice. He had his own family to think of, there was not enough for everyone.

Domenica's father had been an only child, so the family had more than enough land for their needs, plus they had a few patches inherited by his wife. But it would be next summer before they would have a crop, by the time the land was ploughed and prepared for the seeds.

The vegetable gardens were looking desolate and too late for sowing. The market in Atina did have miniature plants but the price was high, four times more than the previous year. Normally at this time they would be harvesting potatoes, but not this year.

Zio Antonio was sitting with Domenica and Peppino. Domenica was asking what she could do, as she had no money.

Zio Antonio asked if she had been to the Post Office in Picinisco, maybe Gaetano had an account there. 'Maybe your father hid something away, have you looked for a Post Office book? Go to the Post Office, take your father and mother's death certificates with you, as well as your own birth certificate and ask if he has an account. Speak with the mayor, maybe he can help you fill in some forms.' Then he went on to say, 'Have you thought of selling some land? There is that piece in the Stirlito – the plot that your mother inherited that borders my land.'

Domenica looked at him. 'Zio who has money to buy land these days?'

'Well,' answered Antonio looking down, 'you can't ask for the kind of money you would have got before the war, but if the price is right, I could buy it.'

'I see,' said Domenica in disbelief, he was obviously not as poor as he had made out. 'I will think about it and let you know'.

After her Zio left, Domenica was thinking and said, 'What do you think, Peppino?'

The boy said, 'I think he wants our land for nothing because we are in dire straits.'

'Yes,' said Domenica, 'I think so too, but I would need to be starving before I sell one inch of our father and mother's land. We will manage somehow. We will show them.'

Peppino was just fourteen years old. He was a tall handsome boy, almost a man. He sat there beside Domenica, thinking.

'Domenica,' he said eventually. 'What am I doing here? We have no animals for me to tend. The coming winter is going to be really hard for us, we need to do something to survive. I have heard that there is work in Atina, rebuilding the roads. I could work and bring home a wage.'

'Yes,' said Domenica. 'It's a good idea for you to go to work, but you are just a boy. Because of your age they will make you work hard, and give you only a pittance. But you are right, even a little will help. Tomorrow we will go to town and ask the mayor if he knows of any work available. Then I will come with you and meet the foreman myself, then he'll know you have a family looking out for you. We will ask the mayor to produce a note saying that you are a good boy and a hard worker.'

'Yes, that's a good idea.' Peppino was excited, happy at the thought of bringing some money home.

'Peppino, I was thinking of something else,' Domenica continued 'It's something that I really don't want to do but it would only be for this winter. What do you think of having Pietro fostered? He is nearly ten years old. He would be fed and clothed and there would be one less at home. I'm saying this because Andrea Pacitti from Villa Latina is looking, he needs a boy to help him on the farm. As I said, I really don't want him to go, I feel as though I am letting Mamma down. What do you think?'

Peppino thought for a moment. He felt the same way as his sister because they both knew that often boys that took up positions as *garzone* were mistreated, abused and made to work long hours. 'He's a tough boy, I think we should ask him. If he wants to go, we will let him. And if he is not treated well, he can come home right away.'

That night they approached Pietro and told him their plan. But, unlike Peppino who was happy to work, because he would bring home money, Pietro understood instantly that he would receive only his keep. He lowered his head and in a childish voice betraying his slim years he said, '*Va bene*, I will try, but if he starts to beat me, I'm coming straight home.'

Pietro prepared to leave. His sister had prepared a bundle of his clothes. He knew that it was best for him to go. The farmer might even send him to school. He knew there was a school in Villa Latina, and he would like that very much. Angelo was still sleeping and Pietro looked at him for a minute, not knowing if he should wake him and say goodbye. They had never been separated, not once.

'No,' he thought, 'he would cry and make a scene.' Pietro picked up his bundle, ready to go.

Downstairs, Peppino said to Domenica, 'What's in the bundle?'

'His clothes, they are all there,' she said.

'No,' he said, 'leave them here and just go with the clothes on your back. We will see if he buys you some clothes and a new pair of boots for the winter. Then you can stay, if not, you will come home.'

Domenica and Pietro laughed, it was so like Peppino to think that way.

CHAPTER 21

Empty Coffers

PICINISCO WAS A small town. The *paese* itself had no more than one thousand inhabitants, but it had many satellites like Valle Porcina bringing the population up to around three thousand *paesani*. The inhabitants of these towns, villages and hamlets liked living close together. They would walk to their fields in the morning and return at night, often including a hard climb.

Picinisco was the hub. On Sundays and on feast days the folk from the surrounding villages would get together and walk to Picinisco. The church bells would call the faithful to Mass. Later the square would be full, and this is where they heard news and unfortunately for some, gossip. If the men had a few extra Lira they would go to the wine cellars and drink a few glasses of wine. Even those with some money, but none to spare, would buy wine and their families would go without.

If the women from the countryside had some produce to spare, they would carry it in their baskets and sell it or barter it for something else.

The town had everything. There was, of course, the mayor who was held in great reverence. He was all that the people knew of politics. They knew nothing about the government, and why should they, government did nothing for them. Ask a random person who the prime minister was, they would not know. They knew about the death of Mussolini, but only because of the war.

Of course, there were the élite of the town. The lawyer, the priest, the engineer. These were the people that sucked the blood out of the poor and illiterate, making sure that they remained ignorant. Often any spare cash they had would end up in their pockets.

The mayor was a man of the people, he had to be voted into office. But he also took advantage of his position. If the country folk wanted something, they would rarely visit the mayor empty handed.

And of course, there were the artisans, the tailor, the cobbler, the funeral director, the carpenter, the builder and all the rest. Then the shop owners. Then the country folk, people who owned a bit of land or rented land and gave half of the produce to the landlord. These people would eat but rarely had money.

The shepherds who lived in the high villages, were at the bottom of the social hierarchy, and were despised and envied in equal measure because to say they were rural people was an understatement. They lived in the wilds just under the snow line and communed with nature in all her beauty and horror. They spent the spring and summer 'up by' and in the harsh winters they would separate their flocks and take up some pasture here or there in the plains, often as far as Cassino and beyond, 'down by'. This itinerant lifestyle, as some saw it, relegated them to the lower orders. But when they returned in the spring, their pockets were full of money and many a jealous eye was cast over them.

The three youngsters were now in Picinisco. They had been to the mayor to ask for a note for both Peppino and Pietro. Domenica said to the boys, 'We will go to the Post Office and ask if father had an account. If he has, then we will celebrate. What would you like, Peppino?'

'I want a new pair of boots, with all the walking back and forth mine have holes in them.'

'And what do you want, Pietro?' she asked her little brother.

'To stay at home with my family.'

Peppino and Domenica exchanged looks of pity for the boy. Peppino pressed the boy to his side and said: 'Just try it, you'll always know your way home. Also, if I get this job in Atina, I will be passing through regularly. I will check up on you. If anyone mistreats you, I will give them a black eye.'

The boy laughed and said, 'And I will give them another black eye.'

The Post Office clerk looked through his files until he found their father's documents and with a deep sigh he said, 'Yes your father has an account with the

Post Office but,' and here the look of happiness on the children's faces faded, 'I'm sorry to say the money has been withdrawn. Your father needed the money for your mother's illness and the war took the rest. I'm sorry.'

The trio realised their plans were unchanged and set off downhill into the valley. When they came to the cemetery, they each knelt and made the sign of the cross, remembering their mother. Their father was buried in Gallinaro, but they never knew where their sister Addolorata was interred. The confusion of the war brought many lamentable oversights.

They went up and down hills and crossed through Colle Posta and soon they were in Villa Latina with its long stretch of straight road followed by the climb to Atina, and finally they reached their destination.

Domenica gave the note to the foreman who would employ Peppino. '*Va bene*, he can start tomorrow,' he said.

Domenica asked how much he would get and how many hours he would have to work. When he told her how much the boy's wage would be, she begged him for more, explaining their plight. He answered that he could not give him a man's wage as he was just a boy. Peppino spoke up, saying that he was strong and would work hard. The man agreed and upped the wage but only by just a little.

On their way home, they stopped at Villa Latina to deliver Pietro to his new home. Domenica and

Peppino had delayed as long as possible dropping him of to keep him close just a little longer. The farmer was glad to have Pietro, he looked him over and could see he was healthy, spirited boy if only a little on the scrawny side.

'You be good to him,' Domenica said. 'Pietro, you work hard for Andrea. Don't be cheeky.'

And with that Peppino and Domenica walked away. Peppino did not have the heart to look back, not wanting to see the look on the boy's face.

Very early the next morning, Peppino set off for his work. Domenica gave him food for the day and also one hundred lira. She said that a man should not go about without a lira in his pocket. With a long walk there and back six days a week, and a day off on Sunday, with his small wage Peppino kept all their heads above water.

And just one week later, as promised, Peppino went to see how his younger brother was. Pietro was so glad to see someone from home. Peppino could see that he had new clothes, but they were not brand new, they were cast offs and were too big for him. The shoes were the same.

Peppino said, 'Tell me, how is the farmer treating you?'

The boy looked at his brother trying not to cry. 'It's ok. I have plenty to eat. I eat at the table with them. I sleep on a couch in the kitchen, but I work from the second I wake until the evening meal at nine o'clock.

I asked Signore Pacitti about going to school and he just laughed. "Do you think I brought you here to feed you and to send you to school?" he said. But it's ok, really it is. I have plenty to eat and I will be all right here.'

Peppino asked the farmer if Pietro could come home one day a month. The boy was missing his family. The farmer begrudgingly agreed.

CHAPTER 22
Domenica Strides Ahead

PIETRO WAS LOOKING forward to tomorrow. It was the one day of the month that he could go home. He would get up early to make the day last as long as possible. But he still had to work today. He was huddled under the blanket. It was time to get up, but it seemed as if he had only slept a few hours. The night before he had been so cold that sleep never came.

He jumped out of bed and quickly slipped into his trousers and then his shoes. The shoes were too big for him, and at first they had caused him blisters. Now his feet had calloused, and they did not hurt anymore, they were just cold, he really needed socks. He pointed this out to the farmer, he rolled his eyes, saying when he went to market in Atina he would buy him a pair in all the different colours.

His first job in the morning was to go to the shed and light a fire under a big black cauldron. He filled it halfway up with water from the well, and then added some potatoes, wormy fruit and bran. He would mix it all, bring it to the boil and then let it cook for half an hour. Once cooled he would feed it to the pigs.

Once the pigs had eaten their fill, he would go back to the house where he would have breakfast consisting of polenta from the night before. As he wolfed it down, he thought that the pigs ate a better meal. But he could not complain because the family was eating the same.

After breakfast, the farmer's two sons departed for school and he was given a large lump of bread and a small piece of cheese tied in a cloth. He would take the goats to graze, the farmer would tell him where to take them with a warning: 'Be careful, do not let the goats nibble on the fruit trees and vines.'

Pietro hated taking the goats for this very reason. They did not like to eat grass from the ground. They wanted to nibble sweeter leaves and herbage well above. So all day long he would be running here and there chastising the beasts. Pietro had grown to hate goats.

Before long, and well before midday he had eaten his bread and morsel of cheese. Because of all the running around he was hungry. He could see Fabio and Luca coming back home from school, for a nice plate of cooked food. He on the other hand, would have to wait for his evening meal.

At this time of the year there was still fruit under the trees that had not completely rotted. The boy would eat some of the fruit which would upset his stomach, but it was a long wait until he guided the flock back home.

Sometimes he would herd the flock home too early and get a good telling off, but how was he to know what time it was?

At the farmhouse there were always jobs to do. The farmer chopped up firewood while Pietro picked up the logs and stacked them. When that was done, it was time again to light the fire to feed the pigs. By this time the sun had set and as soon as that happened, it would turn cold and he would start to shiver. His clothes were really not suitable for winter. He also had a cold and his nose would run which would all end up on his sleeve.

The last job of the day was to stand with a whipping stick in the enclosure and herd the goats towards the farmer. As the goats passed, he would milk them one by one. When this was done, he would help the farmer to filter the milk.

When he could finally retire into the warm kitchen and sit by the fire, he was often completely wet, and steam would come off him as he dried. He watched Fabio and Luca at the table doing their homework.

Then the best time of the day came. A big plate of pasta with tomato sauce was placed in front of him. There was also a big plate of sausages and a bit of pig's ear and bacon to share, the gorgeous fat wobbling in the plate. There were also oily greens and as much bread as he could manage.

His eyes closed quickly after dinner, and he would lay his head on his arms at the table and fall asleep, only to be woken by the farmer's wife when it was time to go to bed or in his case the couch. If the room was warm, he would sleep until morning, but if it was cold he would shiver all night.

The next morning before it was light and anyone was awake, he was off. He walked to the high road and reached Casale where people were just getting up and dogs barked as he passed. He followed the stony track by the river until he rounded a bend and could see Valle Porcina. He walked in, everyone was there, and was so glad, he burst into tears.

He was soon eating, it was still only polenta but it tasted so much better at home with his family. Domenica listened as he spoke of his life as a *garzone*.

The next morning Domenica woke Pietro early. He was huddled close to Angelo and looked so peaceful and happy next to his brother that she was sorry to wake him. She nudged him, telling him that it was time to get up. She sent him off so that he would be on time to start his chores.

She sat at the table and wondered what she should do. She did not want the child to grow resentful. On top of that she felt that she was not keeping the promise that she had made to her mother, on her deathbed, to take care of the children.

At home they were doing what they could. The animals had been herded down the mountain. Two of the goats had two kids each! At Christmas she would be able to sell the three males and keep the female. It was the same for the sheep but fortunately they were all females. The cow should calf by Christmas. Things were getting better, and by the following spring they would be back on an even keel.

The problem was how to get through the coming winter. Peppino's small wage was not enough. The winter in the mountains was bleak. They needed shoes, socks and warm underwear.

The more she thought about it the more she became frustrated. She thought that there must be something she could do. She would go to Picinisco and ask the mayor, ask the priest, ask the doctor if there was any kind of help available. She would survive, but what about the others, what about little Bruno? There must be help for him.

The first person she went to see was the priest but all he could offer was use of some land that belonged to the church. That was fine, but no help at the moment.

She then went to the shop to speak with Filomena. Domenica told her of her dilemma regarding the circumstances of her family. Filomena listened and then remembered that she had heard some men talking about getting a pension because their son had been killed by a land mine. Maybe she could get a pension because she had lost her father?

A light went on in Domenica's mind – 'Well, why not? If other people were getting a pension, why should six orphans not get one?'

She made her way to the Town Hall as fast as possible. She would ask the mayor, she was not ashamed. On the contrary, she had become quite fearless. The mayor was not in, they did not know if he would arrive that day, but she decided to wait, she sat on the bench and waited. It was half past one and the office would close at two o'clock. She would stay there until then.

Early the next morning she was sitting in the same place, on the same bench. The mayor arrived but he was with a man in a fine suit. Domenica waited and waited and eventually the mayor came out again with the same man, he led him to the door and shook his hand. He was about to return to his office when Domenica waylaid him.

'Please, I need to speak with you.'

'Not today, Domenica. Come back tomorrow.'

'No,' she said firmly, 'I have been here since this morning. I need to speak with you now.'

'Be quick then,' he said to her impatiently, 'what do you want now?'

'There are six of us at home, with no father and no mother. There is misery everywhere. We will not survive if you don't get us some help.'

The mayor looked at the near-weeping girl. 'I have told you before, there is nothing I can do. There are many people in the same circumstances. You have family, you have uncles and aunts, ask them for help.'

Domenica answered him, this time she raised her voice just a little. 'They can't help. They have problems of their own. I tell you, if you don't help us in some way we may starve and freeze to death this winter, see how you will feel then. I have heard that people are getting a war pension. Why don't you make an application for us, explaining our situation? We are orphans of the war. Please do something.'

'*Va bene*,' he said, in an attempt to dismiss her. 'Just go home now, I will make an application. But it won't happen soon, it will take time.'

Domenica walked home with a little bit of hope. On the way home she was thinking what she should do with the pig trotters she was carrying in her basket. She could make a pot of soup, a big pot so they could have two plates each. The problem was, what would accompany them? She had no potatoes, no cabbage and only a few beans.

She stopped for a while and sat down on a log at the side of the road. She thought that it was not long before Christmas and those that had sheep had left for their winter homes down-by. Others like herself had no choice but stay at home. The winter in the mountains was bitterly cold, it would snow. There would be nothing for them to do, their only preoccupation would be to keep warm and eat.

She thought a bit longer. She only had the money that Peppino brought home, the poor boy was worn out going to Atina and back every day. He did not spend a lira of his wage. In fact, he still had the one hundred lira that she had given him.

'Let me think,' she said out loud. 'It's only for November and December, up until Christmas, then things will get better. Things will start to look up. In January, the cow will calf, we will have milk again. Then we will slaughter the pig. I know he's only small, but it will sustain us through the winter.'

She would have some money she would sell the kid goats. She had been holding on, resisting the temptation to sell them. She would wait until Christmas when she would definitely get the best price.

Then her thoughts went to Bruno, the poor boy. She needed to get food for him, he was fading away but how could she think about that now?

She stood up and started for home, then all at once she turned around and retraced her steps back to the town. She went to the chemist and explained to Dora that her brother Bruno was not well, so asked if she had something for him. 'Yes, here,' Dora replied, 'give him these vitamins, they will help him.'

Domenica held the bottle tight in her hands and said, 'Dora, you know me, and you knew my father. I can't pay you now, I have no money but at Christmas I will sell three kid goats and I will pay you then.'

Her next stop was Filomena's and again she made the same promise. She filled her basket. She went home.

In the months before Christmas, Domenica would go to Picinisco every week to ask the mayor if he had heard anything about the pension. She would sit on the bench until the mayor spoke with her. His answer every time was, 'No, not yet, come back tomorrow.'

She would go to the shop again and pester Filomena, asking how much she would get for her kid goats and how she could get the best price. The young woman would sit in the square, she loved to look at people, wondering who they were and where they came from.

Soon someone would sit beside her, someone like her who enjoyed chatting. Men, women, young or old, Domenica would talk with anyone. In this way she found out who the strangers were, who their parents were, who their brothers and sisters were, what they did for a living and who they were married to.

One of the men in the square was from Scotland. He was there with his son, who was courting a girl from Fontitune. He was going to marry her, her name was Chiarina. When Domenica heard this, her eyes lit up. She knew Chiarina, this was really something.

Domenica imagined that the people from Scotland must have money. As she was going home, she passed next to them, really close so that they had to move to let her by.

'I'm sorry I did not see you,' she said. 'I was thinking about my kid goats. I must get home and make sure they are fed. The mothers are out grazing but the kids are left in the stable waiting to suckle. They are nice and fat, milk fed only. I am selling them for Christmas. They will make a really nice Christmas dinner for someone.'

The man laughed and said, 'How much do you want for this feast?'

'Well,' she answered, 'I don't know the going rate, but I am selling at thirty lira per kilo. If you want one, I can bring it here for you a couple of days before Christmas.' On and on she went until the deal was made. She had to bring her price down to twenty-five lira, but it was still ten lira more than what Filomena had said.

CHAPTER 23
A Change of Luck

CHRISTMAS WAS JUST around the corner and Antonia wanted to bake something. She remembered her mother would make biscuits for the festive season. The house would have an altogether different aroma which was mouth-wateringly rare. Antonia would help her mother make panettone, *crustole* and biscuits. She knew how to make them now thanks to her mother's shared love of sweet things.

Antonia was the opposite of Domenica, she liked to stay at home. Her pleasure came from keeping the house clean. She was like a little housewife; she liked to cook too but Domenica would not let her, saying that she was wasteful. Domenica would cook herself. Her sister knew that she would help make the food taste a little better, even if it was just plain polenta. She would add a little touch of herbs, garlic, onions and hot pepper – things that did not cost too much or were free. But cooking was Domenica's job, she wanted to know what was coming in and going out of her own kitchen. It comforted her.

The biscuits only needed four ingredients: flour, oil, eggs and sugar. She thought, 'Let's see, I have the first three ingredients, all I need is the sugar.' Domenica would say that it was wasteful to use these ingredients for biscuits, but she was out of the house this morning, she had gone to Picinisco. If she could borrow a cup of sugar she would bake and pay the consequences later. She knew that the boys would be happy.

With a cup in her hand, she first went to her Zia and then to her Zio Antonio. They had no sugar to spare. Eventually she asked Zia Carolina, who had six boys at home and by hook or by crook she made sure that her boys were not short of anything. Her every working moment was dedicated to her family. She had some sugar.

Antonia quickly made her way home and set to work. She sieved the flour, made a well in the middle and added the sugar, eggs and oil. She kneaded it, rolled it flat and then cut it into triangles as custom required. She put them in the oven to cook. The smell while they were cooking was beautiful. She sat at the table and wept. 'Mamma, mamma why did you leave us, I miss you so much.'

As usual Domenica did not return home until late. She would have some news of this and that. Often Antonia did not even listen, or she would lose the thread of what she was saying for goodness sake. Who was she talking about anyway?

Domenica arrived home. She was so excited that she did not even notice the aroma of the biscuits. 'I have some really good news,' she said to Antonia, 'but I will not tell you until Peppino comes home tonight.'

Then she noticed Angelo and Bruno both munching away. 'They look nice, where did you get them?'

'Here,' said Antonia holding out the basket of biscuits, 'you have one, they are good, I made them.'

Domenica took one. 'Hmmm, they are good.' Antonia stood there with her mouth open, the usual tirade about starving families with luxurious appetites never came.

The food was ready, and they were still waiting for Peppino. Domenica sat on the bench outside her front door with Bruno on her lap. The boy was looking better since he had been taking the vitamins, there was more life in him. He would play and laugh sometimes, although at other times she would see a look of horror on his face and he would run to her. She would hold him and rock him, hushing him and telling him that everything was all right. The poor mite. 'It's OK, I'm here.' At times like this she could not deny her thoughts. She would see the horror in a quick flash and she would hold the boy tight, kissing him and reassuring him.

Peppino had arrived and they were sitting around the table. Domenica wished that Pietro was there too, she sat back and said: 'I have something to tell you. I went to Picinisco.' She paused for effect, but no one paid any attention because she always went to Picinisco.

'I went to speak with the mayor,' she bellowed. So what, they thought, that was her favourite pastime. 'But *va bene*, if you don't want to listen, I'm not going to tell you my news.'

Peppino put his spoon down, '*Va bene*, tell us.'

She continued excitedly: 'Do you remember a few months ago I asked the mayor to make an application for us to get a pension, and then every week I went there to remind him so that he would not forget? Well, I went there this morning as usual to remind him. I sat outside on the bench until he showed up. I think he is really sick of me, but I don't care. He can think what he likes. This morning he said that an inspector is coming on Saturday, he wants to see us. We have to go in the morning, he wants to meet us all!'

Peppino was so happy to hear this. Antonia too. Only the boys wondered what the fuss was all about but knew it must be something good because their elders were excited.

Friday night arrived and Peppino came home with Pietro. Domenica had not seen him since his last visit a month before. Peppino looked at Domenica, who was shocked to see her brother in such a state.

'He does look a sorry sight, look at him all dirty, in rags, his cold is not any better, his sleeve caked with snot. That's it, he is not going back.'

Domenica agreed with her brother. How could people be so cruel to a poor orphan boy? From now on, he was staying with them. Even if he had her share of the food. She would go hungry. Domenica felt guilty for letting Pietro go away. She was not only angry with the farmer but also with herself. She washed the boy and Peppino cut his hair. He was still in rags but at least they were clean, his brothers' cast-offs, not some stranger's rags.

CHAPTER 24
Mister De Marco

IT WAS SATURDAY morning and they were all at the Town Hall sitting on the bench, waiting to be called in by the mayor. They were eventually called and entered the office together Domenica carrying Bruno, Peppino by her side and then Antonia, holding the hands of Pietro and Angelo.

The mayor was sitting behind the desk together with a man with a beard and glasses. 'Signore De Marco is going to ask you a few questions,' the mayor said. 'Speak up when you answer.'

Signore De Marco looked at Domenica. 'We will start with you, Domenica. Your name is Domenica Minerva-Crolla?'

'Yes,' the girl said.

'And you are seventeen years old?'

'Yes, sir.'

'And these are your brothers and sister?'

'Yes,' she said pointing at Peppino. 'This is Giuseppe, he is fifteen and this is Antonia, she is thirteen, and the boys are Pietro, ten, Angelo, seven and Bruno is three.' Then she said, looking into the middle distance, keeping her voice from breaking:

'I also had another sister, Addolorata, she would have been sixteen.'

'Domenica, could you ask your brothers and sister to wait outside, I want you to tell me what happened the day your father died.'

The children made their way out. Bruno did not want to go without Domenica and clung to her. The man gave Peppino some coins and said, 'Go and buy ice-cream from Bernice, it's even better than the ice-cream in Rome.'

Signore De Marco looked at Domenica and said to her: 'Now Domenica, take a seat and tell us in your own words what happened that day.'

Domenica sat down and put her feet flat on the ground, the palms of her hands flat on her knees. She took a deep breath to calm down. She knew how important it was for her to recall that day. She could not shake her head and divert her thoughts as usual to the jobs in hand. She had to stop and look at the horror she held in her mind.

'We had moved from Valle Porcina because German soldiers were all over the mountains, stealing livestock from everyone who did not have time to hide them. A few families saved their flock but ours, and most of those of our relations, were taken. My father took us to live in the countryside near Gallinaro. By this time my mother was really very ill spending most of her time in bed, she did not have the strength to stand.

'There was fear everywhere. Fear of raids by the Germans, fear of bombs, fear of planes that flew low in the sky. Some people were put on a train in Sora and taken to Ferenttino never to return.

'My father had rented that house because it had a cellar, and because it was out of the way. But as he said he did not think of danger coming from the sky. There had been heavy bombardment every night that grew closer, we thought it was thunder at first but... We had spent two days and nights in the cellar. That day it seemed quiet, so we left the cellar to get on with our work. Addolorata had taken the cow to graze. The boys were busy with the goats and sheep. My father said that if we saw planes we were to run for the cellar.

'Then all of a sudden, we saw planes flying above us. There was a huge explosion in Gallinaro, so we all ran for home. My father told me to get my brothers and go into the cellar with them while he went to get my mother. In the distance I could see Addolorata running for home. So Peppino, Angelo, Pietro and myself went into the cellar. Then I wondered where Bruno was. I was about to go up to get him when I saw Addolorata at the top of the steps. I shouted to her to get Bruno and I saw her rush towards the house.'

At this point Domenica had to stop. She could not continue, her breath coming in great gasps. She put her hands to her face. 'It's all my fault. If I had not told her to go and get Bruno, she would still be alive today.' Her shoulders shook, she put her head down on the desk and sobbed.

Signore De Marco looked at her in pity and said, 'Take your time Domenica.'

After a moment, she managed to raise her head, wipe away her tears and went on. 'More bombs were falling closer and closer, then there was a whistling sound. A huge explosion, the earth shook, and the house felt as it if was going to fall on top of us, dust and smoke everywhere. We waited a couple of minutes and then Peppino and I ran up the steps to see if anyone was hurt. There was screaming. The door of the house was wide open, and we looked inside.'

Domenica shook her head. 'I didn't want to look inside'. She took a deep breath and continued.

'I ran in, I wanted to help them. Then I stopped, for how could I help? I went to my papa and shook him, I called him but there was no answer. I looked at Addolorata who was screaming, her guts were flowing out of her belly, she was holding them in with her hands. My mother was lying on the floor crawling towards Addolorata. She took an apron and tied it around her waist to keep her intestines from falling out. Then she looked about, saw that her husband was covered with blood and underneath him she saw the legs of her son Bruno, and she passed out. I pulled Bruno out from under Papa, his eyes were open. I picked him up and took him outside, he seemed unhurt.

'Then our neighbours Carmine and Cecilia came to help. Peppino ran to Gallinaro for help and came back with the doctor. My father was dead, a piece of shrapnel had cut an artery, there was blood everywhere. My sister was screaming in pain and fear. They took her to the hospital in Vicalvi where she later died. We still don't know where she is buried.

'My mother was senseless and delirious for days. She screamed and cried. She kept on calling for her husband. She would have moments when her mind was clear Then and she would get angry with God, with the Holy Virgin and all of the angels and saints. She cursed them all.'

The gentlemen looked down at their hands.

'It was about a month later that we packed our things and went back home. Two weeks later my mother died, screaming in pain because there was no more medicine for her.'

There was silence. Tears were running silently down the girl's face. The men were cursing the Fascists who had brought them to this. There was this girl's story, but they had heard many others. Lord have mercy on us all, they thought.

'*Va bene*, you can go now, Domenica,' said the mayor. 'I will speak with Signore De Marco. I will let you know the outcome as soon as I can.' He continued, with a smile, 'There is no need to come here now every week to remind me.' Domenica, bleary eyed but resolute made eye contact with each of the men as she left the room.

'*Grazie* Signor Mayor, *Grazie* Signore De Marco.'

* * *

The mayor's day at the office had come to an end. It was two o'clock and time to go home for lunch. He put on his woollen coat and his trilby hat, looked at himself in the mirror, smoothed his great rich moustache, patted his round belly and pulled his trousers up.

He knew that as soon as he walked through the square, he would be stopped by some poor folk who wanted to speak with him. So today he would sit on the bench under the old tree, the only ornament in the square, because the view was so spectacular, the best in the whole valley. If there was anyone who wanted to speak with him but did not have the courage to come to his office, they could feel free to do so there.

He looked around him. The town had been lucky, just one bomb had hit Picinisco. It had damaged the church in the square, so it was boarded up. Only God knew when the money to repair it would arrive. The main church of San Lorenzo, the larger of the two churches in town, was fortunately still in use.

People passed by him. '*Buongiorno*, Mayor.' He would raise his hat to the ladies that passed by. They would nod their heads and walk on. Eventually he got up to go home. On his way he had many offers for a drink at the bar or a coffee. But he would shake his head, pat his stomach and laugh saying that he was ready for his meal. He walked along and passed an old wine cellar, his old friend Doctor Franco was sitting outside with a drink in front of him.

'Have an aperitif with me.' The mayor sat down, and the doctor ordered a glass of Marsala for him.

'I am in no hurry to get home today,' the mayor sighed. 'I have lost my appetite. The Minerva-Crolla girl – you know her? Domenica? I am making an application for a pension for her and her siblings. Today she had an interview with an official from Rome. She told us the story of what happened to her father and sister.'

'I know the family,' the doctor replied. 'I tended to the mother in the weeks before she died. Terrible business.' The men carried on talking for a while, they both went home for lunch, thankful that their wives and children were home and safe.

CHAPTER 25
Christmas Miracles and New Potatoes

CHRISTMAS CAME AND Domenica sold three of her kid goats. The best price was twenty-five lira per kilo that she got from the Scottish man in the square.

Domenica had some money and the temptation to spend was strong, she wanted to buy things for Christmas but first she had to pay her debts.

'I will get a few things for Christmas,' she thought, 'but I have to be careful, there is still January, February and March to get through.' At the back of her mind was always the thought of the pension. Then everything would be all right.

Domenica went shopping for Christmas. In her pocket she carried only the money that she wanted to spend. She was chatting with Filomena at the same time, looking around to see what she would buy, asking how much this was, how much that was. She finally bought one kilo of sugar so Antonia could bake, six oranges, one for each of them, and one Torrone nougat bar to share.

She went to the emporium and bought twelve pairs of socks, two pairs each. The next stop was at the butchers where she bought one kilo of minced beef to make meatballs. She would add plenty of breadcrumbs and grated pecorino cheese so that there would be plenty for everyone.

That was all, the money had been spent. She walked home, happy.

It was the feast of La Befana, Epiphany Day, the sixth of January, and miracles of miracles, the cow gave birth to twins, two beautiful but tiny calves.

They all stood around the cow. While Domenica was happy that the cow had twins, problem now was that the animal had to suckle two calves. There would not be any milk for them or at least not enough to make cheese.

Christmas faded from memory and the trials of winter subsided. It was April and the calves were growing nicely. The sheep and goats had given birth again. The land had been ploughed and seeded, with both wheat and corn.

It was time to sow potatoes, but no one had any potatoes for seed. Then Domenica, in her usual trip to Picinisco to see the mayor, had heard that in Pescasseroli, in the Abruzzo region, they were giving away seed potatoes for free to anyone who would go and collect them.

That day Domenica spread the news that there were potatoes available. Her next door neighbour, Zio Silvio, said that Pescasseroli was very far away. It was all the way up the mountains, after Forca D'Acero, then down to Opi, and after that a long walk in the valley before reaching the town. It would take at least three days, there and back.

Domenica decided that it was worth the trouble. When other families heard that she was going, then they also sent someone along. In the end a group of ten youngsters, and also a few from the Casale, started the trek, each one carrying a sack and some food for the journey.

It was a beautiful spring day. They were all young and used to hiking, so it was almost like a holiday of sorts.

By daylight they were in Picinisco. At the cemetery they turned down, taking a zig-zag road that went down to the Melfa river and the mill. They then crossed the bridge, then up the hills again on a mule track until they reached Le Caselle where they stopped beside the village fountain to eat their midday meal. Up and up they climbed, passing San Donato, instead of following the road that zig zagged back and forth they took the short cut, a mule track that went straight up. By nightfall they were at the pass. That night they slept in the refuge that they found there, the boys on one side of the cold room and the girls on the other.

In the morning Domenica was ready to go. By this time friendships had blossomed between the girls who walked together. Domenica walked with her cousins and a young man from the Casale, whose name was Sabatino. He seemed to enjoy teasing the girls, especially Domenica.

They soon reached Opi where they stopped to eat and from that point onwards it was all downhill into the high plain. By midday they had reached their destination and found the silo where potatoes were being distributed. Ten kilos each was what they were given, if they wanted more they had to pay.

Domenica was happy with ten kilos, her sack was half full. She balanced it on her head and once everyone was ready, they set off back home. That night they slept in the refuge again, and the next morning they went downhill, not so easy with a load on your head. By the end of the day, by twilight, they were home.

A few days later Domenica got a message from Zio Antonio telling her that the mayor wanted to see her as soon as possible.

'Peppino, Peppino!' she called her brother. 'Quick, get ready, we are going to Picinisco. The mayor wants to see us, it must be about the pension.'

'But I have to go to work,' he replied. 'I can't just take a day off, I will get the sack.'

'If you get the sack it doesn't matter, we are getting a pension. Quick, quick we have to go now.'

Peppino and Domenica sat down on the bench waiting for the mayor. 'Just go in Domenica,' the secretary said, 'the mayor is waiting for you.'

Domenica and Peppino looked at each other, thinking this was unusual, the mayor was waiting for them? Was the news going to be good?' After knocking on the door, they walked straight in where Domenica and Peppino came face to face with John.

CHAPTER 26
And Vera Sang 'We'll Meet Again'

JOHN WALKED TOWARDS them to embrace them. 'I'm so sorry about Gaetano and lovely Addolorata.'

Domenica understood his condolences and said, 'Mamma too' as she held a hand out to Peppino to steady herself. John's presence brought it all back in a flood of memory and emotion.

'This gentleman pilot has come to Picinisco asking for your father,' the mayor said. 'He said that last year he took him in during the bombardment. He had a broken leg, is that right? He stayed with you until his leg was better?'

'Yes,' answered Domenica, 'he came from the sky, he fell from a plane. He is a nice man. Papà liked him. We could not speak with him at first because he spoke English. A friend of my father's Ernesto, from Gallinaro, could speak his language. Between Ernesto, sign language and John speaking a few words of Italian, we got along.' Domenica and Peppino laughed remembering all of their misunderstandings. John looked confused but captured again the warmth with which it was said.

'Let's go to the square for a coffee,' the mayor said. 'We will surely meet someone who speaks English. There is always someone there who has come back from Scotland.'

They sat in the square at a table overlooking the valley and it was almost as if you were on a balcony. The valley spread out before them in its full splendour. Domenica looked into the distance across to Gallinaro. Was it only a year ago when the valley was in darkness?

The sun was warm, it was a pleasure to sit in the sunshine at this time of the year.

John ordered coffee for himself and the mayor. When he asked the girl and boy what they wanted, for reasons of modesty they refused, saying they did not want anything. John asked for a lemon soda and brioche for each of them.

The mayor was called away. John looked at the girl and boy in front of him. He wanted to ask them a lot of questions.

'How is little Bruno?' he asked with a smile.

'Bruno is not too well,' she said.

'What's the matter? Why is he not well?'

Domenica tried to explain but they were soon confused. They just smiled.

The mayor returned with a man, who did not look like he was from Picinisco. 'This is Serafino Capaldi' said the mayor introducing him to John. 'He lives in Edinburgh, in Scotland. He sells fish and chips, but he is one of us from Picinisco. He always returns to where he was born.'

'Look,' he said, extending his hand, 'what a beautiful village.'

Serafino agreed with the mayor, nodding his head and smiling at John.

'Yes, this is a beautiful place, and I always love to come back.' Serafino said in his Scottish accent.

'I will leave you with this gentleman, you can talk,' said the mayor and he walked off.

Serafino looked at the girl. 'You are Domenica, the mayor was telling me about you. I am sorry for your loss.' He looked at John and nodded. 'John, what can I do for you?'

John told him his story and who he was. They spoke about the war. Serafino spoke of his experience in Scotland, how all the Italian men over sixteen were rounded up and taken to the Isle of Man. They spoke of the disastrous sinking of the *Arandora Star*. John spoke of his experience during the Battle of Monte Cassino and the many casualties and deaths. Then he told him of his experience in Gallinaro. He had come back to see Gaetano and his family, and spoke of their great kindness.

Domenica then told John a little of the day when her father and Addolorata died. John asked many questions which Domenica tried to avoid, her emotions would get the better of her. Serafino translated as best he could.

'You said that Bruno is not well, what is wrong with him?'

'As I said, when Papà was killed, Bruno was with him. My father fell on him. I think he was trying to protect him. Papà died and Bruno was unhurt. Bruno now is very quiet, he has bad dreams, and is scared of everything. If he hears a loud bang he screams. He never wants to be alone. He wants me there all the time.'

John was sad to hear this. 'Has a doctor seen him? Is there anything that can be done for him?'

'Doctor Franco said it will take time, but he will be all right, we hope.'

John said that he would like to see the boy and all the other children too. 'I will come to your house. We can go now if that's all right with you. Do you live far?'

'Yes,' said Domenica, 'it's quite a long walk.'

'Is there a taxi we can take?' asked John.

'I will see about that, and I will come with you. I have nothing keeping me just now and I can help with translation.' Serafino went to call Middiuccio.

John enjoyed the ride to Valle Porcina. It was like going back in time. Up the stony rough road, they rattled along. There was no point in speaking as you could not be heard above the roar of the engine. John admired the mountains, the deep valley, the trees with the delicate pale green leaves, new and fresh.

After several bends, they came to an area from where you could see a village perched on the side of the mountain.

'Is that Valle Porcina?' John asked.

'No,' said Peppino. 'That's Fontitune, we have to go down the valley.'

Down they went again with many bends through a forest until they came out of the woods. They could see the village on the edge of what looked like a large dry riverbed with many large boulders.

They stopped and walked to Domenica's house. Outside her house there was a group of children of all ages. Everyone went quiet as they stared at the strangers. Bruno let go of Antonia's hand and ran towards Domenica. He went straight passed her, his arms wide open, his little legs going as fast as they could.

'I like John,' he shouted as John swept him up in his arms.

'And I like Bruno,' John said as he embraced the boy.

John rented a room in Picinisco. He went to Valle Porcina every day as he loved to walk and loved nature. He would immerse himself in the wonderful solitude. He marvelled at the local people he encountered, always chatting to one another. They would stop and openly stare at him.

'Where are you going?' they would ask.

'Valle Porcina,' he would answer.

'What are you going there for?' They knew immediately that he was English. No sane person would walk alone and just for the sake of it.

By the third day they knew who he was and why he was going to the village. News travelled fast. They

to see what she thought about it. And she is just as excited about it as I am. As you know we have no children and I love Bruno so much that I would love to have him as my son. We want to adopt him, legally, you understand. We would give him all the opportunities in life, but most of all we would give him our love as if he were our own son.'

Domenica let Serafino finish. She did not know what to say, the thought had never crossed her mind. Her first instinct was to smile and be happy. What an opportunity, and such good luck for Bruno!

'Domenica, please do not say anything now. Think about it, speak with your brothers and sister. One thing though Domenica. I already love Bruno and my wife will love him too. You must not worry about that.'

They sat in silence for a while, each lost in their own thoughts. Then John and Serafino got up to go.

CHAPTER 27
The Adoption

DOMENICA'S MIND WAS in turmoil. She sat at the table with Antonia beside her. They were talking about Bruno and what they should do. Antonia looked at her sister. Domenica wanted to speak with Peppino, but she had to wait until the evening when he returned home.

'I am going to speak with Zio Antonio,' she said. After very little thought, her Zio agreed that it would be good for the boy, as he would get an education and maybe John could also help the rest of the family.

That night she said to Bruno, 'Do you want to go away with John? John will get you new clothes and shoes. He will buy you sweets every day and he will give you toys to play with. Would you like that?'

The boy cuddled into Domenica, put his thumb in his mouth and went for Domenica's ear and, half asleep, he said, 'No, I want to stay with you.'

That night after they had eaten, Bruno was asleep. The rest of them were sitting around the table talking. Domenica, Peppino and Antonia were in agreement to let Bruno go, although they would miss him and hate to part with him, but they knew it would be for his own good.

But Pietro did not agree with them. 'He is not going anywhere!' he shouted, standing up. 'He is staying here with us. He is not going to be a *garzone*. It's horrible being a *garzone* – cold, hunger, beatings, you get treated like a dog. It's better to eat bread and onion with the family, not bread and cheese somewhere else where nobody cares for you. We can all eat a little less so there is enough for everyone.' He burst into tears and went to sit next to Bruno. The rest of the family looked at each other speechless.

The next morning, after the animals had been milked, Pietro and Angelo herded the flock out to graze. Pietro took Bruno by the hand and led the boy away with him. Domenica searched for the child, but she could not find him anywhere. He didn't normally go far so she walked up the hill for a better look. From there, she could see her two brothers, Bruno being led by Pietro.

She sat on a boulder. 'Mamma! Papà! What should I do?' she thought to herself. She thought of her mother, holding her hand, asking her to promise to take care of the poor orphan children. She had promised her, but what was for the best?

Bruno was just beginning to get better. He was too young to think of what was good for him. As far as he was concerned, it would just represent another separation from the family. He did like John, he liked to be with him, and John made him happy by playing with him and giving him sweets, but to go away with him was something completely different. It was not the same as his own family.

But what else was there for him here? In fact, for all of them, it was a constant struggle to survive. None of them had been to school, it was too late for her, but at least the boys could go. She would speak with Peppino later on and sleep on it. When John returned, she would tell him that she needed more time.

The next day John stayed all day playing with Bruno and talking with Domenica. He said to her that he had his return train ticket, there were only seven days left before he had to go. But if Domenica agreed with the adoption of Bruno, then he would not leave. His wife would come to Picinisco so that Domenica could meet her. She would like her, she was a nice person, a good woman. He had a job to go back to, but he said that this was more important, so they would stay as long as it took.

John had met the family next door. He had a large family like everyone else in these mountains. They would sit outside and ask John questions about everything. John was speaking to one of his daughters, Paola, a pretty girl with a head full of curly hair that she found difficult to keep under control. She was a lively, bright eyed girl, full of fun. She enjoyed teasing John and asked about his wife. Was she pretty? Was she elegant? Was her hair short? There was no end to the questions and always plenty of laughter.

Paola had a boyfriend who came to see her often. John had met him as well as many of the youngsters in the area. He had a quick intelligent look about him, his eyes were a piercing blue colour. John enjoyed watching

Paola torturing this young man, blowing hot and then cold. One minute she would act shy with him and the next she was a temptress. She had him spinning.

Sometimes, to get away from her, Paola's boyfriend would chat with John – somehow they managed to understand each other. It turned out that Raffaele was related to Serafino Capaldi, they were cousins. Raffaele had been a prisoner of war in a German prison camp, he could even speak a little German. John could also speak a little bit of German, so the men would talk as best they could about the war.

When this happened Paola would get into a mood, asking Raffaele if he had come to see her or John. She would then laugh and go inside the house and Raffaele would follow. John watched, thinking: poor Raffaele. He went with the hope of a kiss. If there was silence in the house then he had been lucky, if not he could hear him getting his face slapped.

Three days had passed. Domenica thought that she had to say something to John. At first, she thought that her answer would be yes. It would be hard for them all, not just for Bruno. But in the long run it would be best for the child. She had made her decision.

But then she watched Bruno. He seemed better, but was he? He would go with John quite happily, but he would always look for his sister. If John wanted to go for a walk, he would go just so far and then cry because he wanted to go back home. If he wanted to sleep, he would sit on her lap. As soon as he awakened, he would be scared and shout, "Menica.'

The day after was Sunday and Peppino was at home. Domenica had a nice meat sauce cooking for Sunday lunch and it filled the house with a beautiful aroma. They sat at the table. They were quiet, everything had been said, they had nothing left to say. They heard Bruno shouting, 'I like John', and they knew he had arrived.

John walked into the house holding Bruno by the hand. He knew that he was getting a decision today. Tomorrow he would go home, or he would send a telegram to his wife to join them.

He sat down, looking at the faces of the children around the table.

'If Bruno was not so attached to me,' Domenica began, 'if what had happened to him had not happened, if he was not so fragile, it would be all right. But I am scared that if he is separated from us, he would be very upset, and would not get over it. I know that you love him as your own. I know that he would have every opportunity in life. But we cannot part with him, it's not just my decision. We all agree. I'm so sorry.'

John was heartbroken but he said no more and just nodded his head. 'I understand, Domenica.'

He stood up to go and looked around the table. He picked Bruno up to hug him. 'I like Bruno,' he said. He put him down and went away.

Domenica ran after him. 'Wait, John.' But John just raised his hands and walked on in tears. Domenica stood with Bruno by her side and shouted, 'A Dio, John.'

CHAPTER 28

She Was a Determined Woman

AFTER JOHN LEFT that day, everyone was subdued. Peppino felt resolute, he felt sorry for John like everyone else did, but in his mind he knew they had done the right thing. He went to work with more vigour and worked hard. Soon, when his birthday came, he would earn more money to take home to his brothers and sisters. He was glad that when he returned home that night Bruno would still be there, not another void in their lives. He thought of his parents and his sister Addolorata, who he missed very much. He had been very close to her, she was his best friend, they were close in age and also in temperament.

When he left for work, he could see that Domenica had that worried look on her face that he was so familiar with. 'Be happy,' he said to her. 'We did the right thing. Just think how you would have felt to see Bruno walk away crying and this morning him not be here.'

Domenica was not so sure that they had made the right decision for Bruno. She kept thinking of all the lost opportunities. But she shook her head and did not want to think about that now.

She thought that she would go to town to see the mayor, that always cheered her up. She loved nothing more than to go for a walk – but then she thought that she should avoid Picinisco today as John would be there and she really could not face him once again with his sadness.

So, she took Bruno and walked down the road, she would surely meet someone for a chat. As soon as anyone saw her, they came out to ask how John had taken the news. How do they think he felt? they asked. Everyone she saw gave their opinion regarding the family decision. This was not what Domenica wanted to hear. She was trying not to think about it.

As she walked past Carolina's house, she noticed that Carolina had not come out to join the speculation. Carolina was one to mind her own business, not wasting time when she could be doing something for her boys, so Domenica did not often look in on her, but she stopped this time to see if her youngest boy was there so he could play with Bruno.

She was, and the two boys were soon playing together. Carolina looked at the boys playing and said: 'You did the right thing. I could never part with one of my boys, not even for a million lira. Now, would you like some tea?'

Domenica nodded. She asked Carolina what she was sewing, as she had material on the table. Carolina answered that she was making a shirt for Francesco, for his first holy communion. Francesco was the same age as Angelo. Angelo should really be taking the same sacrament – even Pietro had not received his first communion.

'It will be next year for both of the boys,' Domenica said with a sigh. 'It's not possible this year. But by next year everything will be better.'

* * *

Domenica had been waiting for news about her application for a pension. She was angry with the mayor for taking so long. Six months had already passed.

'That's it,' she thought. 'I will go there every day and kick up a fuss.' She did not care. It was probably true what people said, if there was nothing in it for them, nothing would be done.

Her neighbour, Zio Silvio, said to Domenica: 'Kill one of your kid goats and take it to the mayor if you want something done.' But the thought of parting with her prized animals and simply giving one away was too much to bear.

No, she decided, she would go to his office and make a scene in front of everyone. She would say that they were starving, six orphans and nobody cared, least of all the mayor. She would say it out loud in the square. She thought that perhaps she could go to see the mayor on Sunday, with the rest of the family. Maybe he would be spurred into action if he saw them all together, in rags, but she did not want to wait until Sunday. She wanted to go now.

Domenica walked briskly, her black skirt swishing around her ankles. Her short-sleeved blouse was also black. She wore a headscarf on her head, tied at the back, and, of course, a black apron. No country woman would be seen without an apron. It was usually made of cotton with a bit of lace around the edges. Domenica was in black, in mourning. Domenica did not realise but she made a striking figure striding down the square. She would show them. She did not look left or right, she went straight to the Town Hall and walked straight in.

'I want to see the mayor,' she said.

'Yes,' said the woman behind the desk. 'I think he wants to see you too. I will tell him you are here.'

'Tell him I am here and I don't want to wait all day. I have five hungry children at home, and I don't know what I am going to feed them.'

She was a determined woman. The mayor called her in straightaway, which made Domenica think that her plan had worked. She walked in holding herself upright, ready for a fight. As soon as she entered his office the mayor stood up and was smiling at her and asked her gently to sit down. 'Oh, how can I be angry with him if he's smiling,' she thought.

'I have really good news for you,' he said.

CHAPTER 29
A Daze

DOMENICA WALKED HOME in a daze. She could not believe it. She kept shaking her head, pinching herself. Could it all be just a dream? She looked in her basket and they were all there – six Post Office books.

Now she wished that she had gone to Filomena to buy something as a treat for all of them. But when she passed the shop, she knew that she did not have a lira in her pocket. The thought that she could get something and pay later had not crossed her mind. She remembered how uncomfortable she had felt when she had been in debt to Filomena, and she swore that she would not get into debt again. If she had the money she would buy, otherwise she would do without. But things were different now, she would have money every month.

She could not wait to get home to tell everyone.

'I have news', she said looking at Peppino. She took the six books out of her basket. 'One each.' She smiled, bursting with joy. 'These are our pension books. Money goes in every month. You will all get a pension until you are eighteen years old. The mayor said I will get one until I am twenty-one because I am the eldest.'

Everyone was happy to hear this. No more hard times. After they had all calmed down, Domenica continued: 'Now my darlings, this pension means that we won't go hungry again, but we still have to be careful. Everyone must still do their chores and we have to save money, so that we can rebuild our flock. We are shepherds, we must have a flock. Then Peppino can stop slaving away from home and next year Pietro and Angelo can have their First Communion. We will spend a little of our pension and save some.

'Now we will have a treat tomorrow. I will go to the Post Office and get some money. What do you want? Tell me, tell me!'

They all told her what they wanted. Once they had all calmed down again, she pulled out a sealed envelope from the basket.

'This is from John,' she said.

They looked at it. Should they open it? They knew that even if they did, they could not read it. They thought of calling on Zio Silvio to read it for them but Peppino said no.

'We don't want everyone to know what it says,' he said, firmly. 'Let's keep it, and if we see Serafino on Sunday in Picinisco we will ask him to read it. After all, it will be in English.'

The following day, Domenica went to the emporium to buy some new clothes for them all. She would get shoes just for Sundays. On Saturday she made all the children stand in a tub and she personally made sure that they were all clean.

She did the same herself. She took her time and had a good long soak. Antonia poured water on her head until her hair was squeaky clean and she felt as if her worries were being washed away. She sat there, thinking. The day after she would put away her mourning clothes and wear her new ones. But was that enough to regain her lost youth?

'I must,' she said shaking her head, 'but I will not think about that now.' She put water by the fire for her brother to wash when he came home.

On Sunday they all put on their new clothes and walked to Picinisco where they went to Mass. They sat in the square afterwards, each eating an ice cream. Domenica was looking for Serafino. She could see him talking in a group of men. Sunday in the square was the time for news and all the voices together made quite a chorus.

He must have noticed her looking at him because after a while he went over to speak with them. They talked about John and how sad it was to see him go and then Domenica held out the letter and asked him to read it.

When Serafino opened the letter, five thousand lira fell out of the envelope. They gasped. He gave the money to Domenica who she just stared at it. Then Serafino read:

Serafino, I'm sure it will be you reading this letter and I didn't get a chance to say good-bye and thank you for all your translations. So, thank you and good luck.

*

Dear Domenica, Peppino, Antonia, Pietro, Angelo and Bruno,

First of all, I want to say that this war has been terrible, so many people died, including so many innocents like your father and sister. I am one of the lucky ones, I managed to get home and found my loved ones waiting for me unharmed.

I was lucky to have met your father. He was a good man, and so clever and resourceful. I believe these qualities have passed to you, Domenica. How can a girl as young as you be so wise, so unselfish, so loving to her brothers and sister while carrying the responsibility for them all?

I'm happy that I came to know you all, especially little Bruno. My heart is broken that he will not be my son. But you are right, maybe the change would be too much for him.

There is something else I want to say. My wife and I never thought of adoption before and maybe this experience has opened our minds to what is possible and all the joy adoption could bring. Maybe there is another Bruno for us, God willing. Tell Bruno that I like him very much. I hope we may meet again.

I am leaving my address, if you ever need something, write to me. If I can help you, I will. Just as you helped me in my hour of need.

May God bless you all.
With genuine affection,
John

PART THREE

New Beginnings, 1954–55

CHAPTER 30
Domenica Gets Married

DOMENICA WAS IN her bed, her eyes open. She had woken early and couldn't sleep, she was nervous and felt agitated. Her wedding day had arrived.

It was the middle of September, the nights were now cold in the mountains. Antonia was snuggled up to her. She looked at her beloved sister and for a moment she thought of her other unfortunate sister, Addolorata, but she shook her head, resolved to not dwell on sadness today.

The night before Antonia had helped her bathe, covering her body in warm olive oil from head to toe and then with a rough cloth, scrubbed until her skin was pink and glowing. She then lay in the warm perfumed bath for a long soak, went to bed hoping to get a good night sleep.

Domenica nudged her sister. Domenica slipped out of bed and went to the mirror to look at herself and was surprised, it must be true that beauty comes from the happiness within, her eyes were luminous, her hair shiny and her skin glowing.

In the kitchen, everything was ready, the house clean, chairs laid out for the guests and the table covered with a white linen cloth had an abundance of bread and wine, their best Pecorino cheese and, an extra extravagance, Parmeggiano and Provolone. Antonia had made trays of *le crustole* which no celebration would be without, delicate ribbons of fried pastry made into bows and covered with sugar and honey.

They had also invited Carmine and Cecilia, Ernesto and his wife to the wedding. As tradition required, she was waiting for her Sabatino to arrive with his parents. At last Sabatino's mother came into her room with a white box which she opened to show a beautiful wedding dress, white and pure. She slipped into its silky softness, then Sabatino's father presented her with a small box, inside was her wedding gift of gold earrings, necklace and bracelet.

Sabatino waited eagerly outside, trembling with anticipation. He couldn't believe that at long last this day had come, and he would soon see his bride. His eyes fixed on the front door, waiting. When Domenica appeared on the arm of her brother, the sun shone on her white dress, she was so beautiful. Their eyes locked and they smiled at one another. He stepped toward her and a poesy of roses in her hand and offered her his arm.

CHAPTER 31
The New Bride Returns Home

DOMENICA WALKED ALONG the rough road that followed the side of the Rava. She walked tall and proud, her arms swinging by her side. She felt as though she wanted to run, just for the sheer joy of it.

She had been married for one month. She had never known such happiness. She loved her husband and he adored her. After all these years of waiting, their love was now fulfilled. To lie in each other's arms was true bliss. They lived with his parents. It was as if night would never come and morning always came too early.

He would say as he rolled out of bed, 'It's already morning.' There were things to do but she would hold on to him and ask him not to go. He would tear himself away. There was milking to be done and if he was late, he would get a dirty look from his father. 'You stay in bed and wait for me. Once the milking has been done, I will come back.'

She lay there waiting for him and when he came back smelling of the stables, she couldn't have cared less.

She felt light-headed and carefree, it was as if she had never known such freedom. She was no longer the one that everyone turned to, after twelve long years of solving everyone's problems. Now her mother and father-in-law decided everything, and Sabatino was of an age where he knew how to run the show. She took a back seat and let everything be. Her new family were happy with her. Although Sabatino's mother said to him, 'Doesn't Domenica like to chat; Domenica likes to gossip; Domenica likes to go walking.' She thought he should tell her that she wasted too much time but Sabatino laughed. It would be like telling the Rava river to stop flowing. He liked her just the way she was. He knew her deep down and that she was the woman that he admired and respected.

Domenica could see the beech forest, which was just starting to turn russet. Soon the people that were moving to their winter homes down-by would be thinking of departing. The closer she climbed towards Valle Porcina, she could feel the difference, it was colder there. This was the first time she had retuned since she had been married. She had left them to fend for themselves. She did not want Sabatino thinking that she could not wait to get back. That morning when she told her husband that she was going to Valle Porcina, he laughed and said he was wondering how long she would last. He hugged her and said everything was under control and she could take all day.

'What will your mother say?' she exclaimed.

'Don't mind what she says. Just worry about what I say,' he replied and laughed again. 'I will join you as soon as I have finished bringing in the bales of hay.'

Soon, with her long stride, she was nearly there. She could see Bruno coming to meet her, and she was so glad to see him.

'I have some grapes and figs,' she told him and held out her basket for to him to carry home. As she walked through the village, people came out to greet her, asking her if she was enjoying married life. What some mentioned made the young woman blush.

Domenica walked on without stopping because she wanted to get home. She walked into the kitchen and as she did, Antonia and Giovanni sprang apart. Domenica laughed.

'Ha, when the cat's away the mice will play.' But Domenica was a changed woman. She hugged her sister, giving her a squeeze. She was happy and she spread her joy around. Antonia looked at her in wonder and was amazed at the change.

It was midday and they sat around the table; Giovanni stayed to eat with them. They talked about Antonia's wedding – the date had been set for just before Christmas.

As usual, the young folk came to sit outside the house, everyone in a festive mood. A new bride had returned home for the first time. If Domenica still had her parents, it would have been a celebration, a happy occasion, with a mother often in tears to have her daughter under her roof again. There would be invitations to close family, feasting and music.

This for the time being was a low-key event, but the word soon spread that the new bride was home. By late afternoon friends and neighbours came to greet her and her beloved Sabatino had arrived. They ate, danced and sang into the night.

CHAPTER 32
Canneto

THE SUMMER WAS warm and mellow. Domenica, as usual, went to Valle Porcina to make bread for the boys. They managed very well, but one of the things they could not do was make bread, so once a week, as she had promised her mother, she went to bake for them.

While the dough was rising, she walked to Peppino's house to visit Resti. She walked into the kitchen but Resti was not there so she called up the stairs and got an answering call from Resti that she would be down in a minute.

Domenica looked around – everything was neat and clean with flowers on the table. The house was only two rooms, a kitchen and a bedroom above. It was looking really cosy. They had bought a couple of pieces of furniture from down-by. She smiled. She was happy for them.

Domenica sat at the new table. Resti came down to join her, looking really well. Resti was expecting a baby.

They were soon talking about 'La festa di Canneto'. The Feast of the Madonna of Canneto was the biggest festa of the year and everyone that could, would go.

The Sanctuary of Canneto was famous throughout La Ciociara for its black Madonna. People made annual pilgrimages seeking solace or like so many before them in pursuit of healing for themselves or a loved one. It was a long walk to Canneto, at least five hours through steep mountain passes, and many of the pilgrims had come from much further afield. They would pass through singing hymns and repeating Hail Marys deep into the night. Some made the trip on foot from as far away as Naples. It was a beautiful and peaceful place and home to a solitary white Basilica perched on a promontory close to a mountain spring. This was the source of much of the water in the valleys below.

'It would be nice if we all went together on the eighteenth,' Domenica said to Resti. 'We could get a message to Antonia and Giovanni to come too. What do you think?'

'Yes,' responded Resti, 'that's a great idea. I will talk with Peppino to see if he is off that day.'

It was all arranged, and the eighteenth soon came. Domenica and Sabatino had everything ready the night before, so they could set out early in the morning. By five o'clock they were already at Valle Porcina.

Domenica was carrying a giant basket full of food. Sabatino was carrying bread and wine. Everyone carried something. Pietro looked comical, with a watermelon strapped to his back; and, of course, Angelo brought his little accordion. They were to meet Antonia and Giovanni there, and they were sure Antonia would have made sweet treats.

As they passed through Fontitune, Resti and Peppino stopped for a while at Zia Maria's, where they enjoyed some wine and biscuits on the terrace. It seemed the whole world was passing by her little house. The voices of the faithful raised in joyful hymns and the pacemaker shouting *E viva Maria*! Hail Mary! at the top of his lungs. These salutations and distant singing could be heard throughout the valley as the pilgrims were now nearing their destination.

Domenica sat at the end of the pew, the Madonna with her sky-blue dress encrusted with jewels at the top of the nave. People were going up to touch her and genuflect before her, while others pinned money on ribbons hanging around her robe. Some even took the gold chains from their neck and slipped it over the head of the Madonna to lay on her breast with many others.

Domenica looked at her family sitting on the bench beside her. They were all there, all of them looking beautiful and healthy.

She was remembering that day in Gallinaro in the church of San Gerardo when she had a Mass said for her Father and Sister. She remembered the photo of her father with the cow. She thought of her mother and her final words to her. She reached for Sabatino's hand and closed her eyes. 'See, Mamma and Papà,' she thought, 'We are all here.'

'*Eternal Rest grant unto them*, Oh Lord, and let perpetual light shine upon them,' she said, holding back the tears. There have been enough tears now.

CHAPTER 33
La Ballarella

ON THE LUSH grass in the shadow of the church, they had their picnic. Families chose the same spot each year to be sure to encounter their relatives and friends. A channel of ice-cold spring water crossed the clearing with little bridges here and there. Stalls selling souvenirs and statues of La Madonna were everywhere. The distant calls of Hail Mary! continued as new arrivals came thick and fast, holding heralds with the name of their parish or paese emblazoned in gold script. The festival was in full swing as they sat to eat their food, and it was such good food: stuffed roast chicken, stuffed peppers, frittata, salad, beans and their best cheese and ricotta. Antonia also brought biscotti and panettone.

Then they ate the watermelon that Pietro had put to cool. There was plenty of wine and everyone they knew was offered a glass. Angelo got out his little accordion after lunch and the dancing began.

Unusually for her, Domenica and Sabatino were the first up for *La Ballarella*. Her family watched, clapping in time with the music. Domenica used her fan and her eyes as she moved through the first coquettish parts of the dance with her husband.

She shimmied this way and that turning to look over her shoulder. 'No, no, no,' she said wagging her little finger at him. He beckoned her as she twirled, jarring her hips in sharp little bursts, the tiny moves flicking her skirt tails.

Clapping her hands now just next to her face, Sabatino mirrored her moves as they turned into and away from each other in rhythm. Smiling and laughing as the dance reached its crescendo. She thought, I'm happy now thank God, and I want the world to know it.

A note from the author

MY FIRST BOOK, *The Wee Italian Girl,* is a memoir of my early life in the village of Fontitune in the Italian Apennines. My family left Italy in the 1950s, when I was eight, to start a new life in Scotland but Fontitune never left me. The book was intended to be a document for other Scottish Italians – and Italians around the world – who left but will always remember, who will always be connected to their roots. We are the last generation to have memories of a place and era that has now gone, and whenever I meet others like me, especially those who grew up in Fontitune, the conversation always goes back to when we were children. The village was full of life back then, so many children and families making a living in that remote place at the side of a mountain. Some people may say we were '*povera gente*', poor people, but as far as I am concerned we were not poor, we were happy. I think we were the lucky ones.

In 1965, years after my family left Italy, we returned to Fontitune for a wedding. My cousin, Giacitta, was marrying a local man called Angelo. It was at this wedding that I met Angelo's brother, Bruno and we fell for each other at once. After three years, he came to Scotland and we were married. *The Wee Italian Girl* is my story, *Domenica* is Bruno's story.

Over the years, I have come to know and love Bruno's family as my own. I have heard the stories of their time during the war, the hardship that followed. And I have seen how they have grown together since. I have heard the stories of his father and mother and their sister Addolorata, the story of John the English pilot. I have seen for myself the photo of their father Gaetano with the cow, still there on display in the church of San Gerado. I know that, one summer, Peppino and Bruno had the remains of their father moved to the cemetery in Picinisco so that he could lie next to his wife, Maria. They sadly could find no trace of their sister Addolorata.

In October 1997 Bruno's brother, Peppino was nearing the end of his life. Lying in bed one day, with me sitting beside him, I could see that he kept looking out of the window. I asked him what he was looking at. And he replied: 'You see that mountain in the distance? That is the peak of La Meta. How many of my footsteps have passed on that mountain, as man and boy. I would have liked one last walk on its plateaus and one last climb to the peak, to look down to see the flock of sheep grazing and to have one last drink at the mountain spring.'

* * *

If you read both *The Wee Italian Girl* and *Domenica*, they bring Fontitune back to life. The village is now almost uninhabited, some have immigrated to the UK, to America and Canada or others moved down from the mountains. Those that immigrated to the USA and Canada come back at least once to Italy in their lifetime to show their children their roots. Folk that moved to the UK return often, spending their retirement partly in their hometown, as I do. My children, Maria and Remo, love Italy; my grandchildren Lia, Matteo and Erica love it even more. They can't wait for the summer holidays to go to Italy. I am so grateful for this because although my children and grandchildren are British citizens born in Edinburgh and their first language is English, we are well integrated in my new home and I am glad that they love Italy, too.

Bruno, the youngest of his siblings, was particularly close to his sister, Domenica. And Bruno always held a special place in Domenica's heart. So, when in January 2016, Domenica, at the age of ninety, was dying, Bruno and I went to Italy to see her. It was late at night when we arrived and we went directly to the hospital. Bruno sat beside her and held her hand. She opened her eyes to look at him and within three hours she had passed away.

One day, I thought to myself, *I will write down her story, their story*. And I did.

Luath Press Limited

committed to publishing well written books worth reading

LUATH PRESS takes its name from Robert Burns, whose little collie Luath (*Gael.*, swift or nimble) tripped up Jean Armour at a wedding and gave him the chance to speak to the woman who was to be his wife and the abiding love of his life. Burns called one of the 'Twa Dogs' Luath after Cuchullin's hunting dog in Ossian's *Fingal*.

Luath Press was established in 1981 in the heart of Burns country, and is now based a few steps up the road from Burns' first lodgings on Edinburgh's Royal Mile. Luath offers you distinctive writing with a hint of unexpected pleasures.

Most bookshops in the UK, the US, Canada, Australia, New Zealand and parts of Europe, either carry our books in stock or can order them for you. To order direct from us, please send a £sterling cheque, postal order, international money order or your credit card details (number, address of cardholder and expiry date) to us at the address below. Please add post and packing as follows: UK – £1.00 per delivery address; overseas surface mail – £2.50 per delivery address; overseas airmail – £3.50 for the first book to each delivery address, plus £1.00 for each additional book by airmail to the same address. If your order is a gift, we will happily enclose your card or message at no extra charge.

Luath Press Limited
543/2 Castlehill
The Royal Mile
Edinburgh EH1 2ND
Scotland
Telephone: +44 (0)131 225 4326 (24 hours)
email: sales@luath. co.uk
Website: www. luath.co.uk